Children's
Magazines:
AN INTERNATIONAL SURVEY

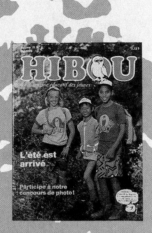

Children's Magazines:

AN INTERNATIONAL SURVEY

ORGANIZED BY *Cricket*

CONTENTS

7 INTRODUCTION

11 EUROPE

Albania • 12
Austria • 13
Bulgaria • 15
Czechoslovakia • 17
Denmark • 24
East Germany • 25
West Germany •· 26
Finland • 37
France • 43
Great Britain (England) • 56
Great Britain (Wales) • 60
Greece • 61
Hungary • 63
Iceland • 68
Italy • 70
Malta • 81
Netherlands • 83
Norway • 88
Poland • 89
Spain • 91
Sweden • 96
Switzerland • 99
Yugoslavia • 106

111 USSR

127 AFRICA

Congo • 128
Egypt • 129
Ghana • 130
Kenya • 132
Nigeria • 133
South Africa • 135
Tanzania • 139
Zaire • 140

141 MIDDLE EAST

Iran • 142
Iraq • 152
Israel • 153
Syria • 156
Turkey • 157
United Arab Emirates • 1

161 FAR EAST ASIA

People's Republic of
China • 162
Hong Kong • 178
India • 181
Japan • 189
Korea • 192
Mongolia • 193
Singapore • 195
Taiwan • 200
Thailand • 206

207 AUSTRAL-ASIA

Australia • 208
Indonesia • 211
New Zealand • 212

213 NORTH AMERICA

Canada • 214
USA • 222

247 CENTRAL & SOUTH AMERICA

Bolivia • 248
Guatemala • 249
Uruguay • 250
Venezuela • 252

253 INDEX

Children's Magazines - Bridges to Books

The exhibit of children's periodicals from all over the world is the first of its kind in the history of children's literature and children's magazines. It is also a first in the twenty-two year history of IBBY Congresses.

A small group of American children's literature people who had gathered during the festive 20th anniversary IBBY Congress in Japan to brainstorm the 1990 U.S. Congress suggested devoting part of the program to the badly neglected field of children's periodicals. Several months later, the IBBY 1990 program chair asked if I'd be willing to organize an exhibit of children's magazines from as many countries as possible.

It was a bigger job than I could have anticipated! We began by putting together a questionnaire that would give us the most important information about each magazine, such as editorial mission, focus, history, and content. We asked for quality magazines for 3- to 16-year-olds, not for comics or children's newspapers. Through IBBY National Section membership lists and with the help of international agencies and the staff of the International Youth Library in Munich, we collected names and addresses of children's magazines, their publishers and editors. Soon, hundreds of letters containing questionnaires were flying to countries all over the world.

Gathering information about the magazines and getting copies for the exhibit was a long and difficult process. Many letters were returned and had to be sent out again and again ... but, finally, magazines began to arrive. Although it was impossible to obtain every single periodical from every single country, the resulting exhibit of 270 children's magazines from 55 nations is a good and solid international representation

Why did we find it important to organize this exhibit and to discuss children's magazines in the framework of an International Congress? There are many reasons, but the most important one is that magazines with their immense variety of content seem to be the one form of reading best suited for our fast-paced times. "Magazine" literally means "a storehouse for various goods," in this case a mixture of different literary genres, features, activities, illustrations, and photographs. The relatively short stories, the variety of subject matter, and the lively format attract children to reading, children who have many different interests and tastes and who may shy away from books. Most magazines also have a variety of reading levels to suit different age groups. Beautiful illustrations and photographs, often in color, may make a magazine attractive even to reluctant or nonreaders. Indeed, magazines with their abundance of short stories, different literary genres, poetry and rhymes, etc., are one of our best vehicles for introducing children to the world of literature and for helping them develop into enthusiastic and lifelong readers. Magazines are truly bridges to books and bridges to literacy.

Another important role magazines play for children everywhere is that they build a community of readers. Children who read magazines are in touch with the world as well as with each other and with the editors of "their" magazines. Most children's periodicals publish and answer their readers' letters and encourage a constant stream of feedback from their audience. Because of this interaction with children, this close reader-editor relationship, magazines are never fixed or static. They are "alive," ready for change, expansion, dialogue, communication, and adjustment to their readers' wishes. And because of this intimate relationship with their audience, magazine editors have valuable data about the interests, tastes, and preferences of today's children. Therefore, periodicals can play an important role in shaping the way societies look at and interact with their youngest members.

Most children's magazines also provide a vital creative outlet for their young readers -- a chance for children to explore the world of the arts firsthand. A great majority of the magazines we reviewed sponsor creative writing, drawing, or other contests and encourage children's efforts by publishing the prize-winning stories, poems, essays, or drawings. Such contests provide many children with their only chance of exercising and developing their natural writing or other artistic abilities.

Most periodicals feature handicrafts, recipes, puzzles, and riddles, and help capture children's interest with other fresh and lively activities. Many recommend good books to read on either general or specified topics.

Most of the magazines for younger children include short picture stories, ready made for parents to read aloud and so stimulate a first interest in story and reading and in imaginary worlds. Preschoolers learn to make associations between the written word and the pictures that accompany a story and gain a rudimentary understanding of colors, shapes, and aesthetics.

Another important consideration is that magazines are *convenient* for today's busy and often working parents, who don't have to make trips to bookstores or libraries or worry about which books to

choose. In periodicals, the selection is already made for them, a
careful selection, always full of exciting surprises. The magazine
arrives at their homes once a month, eagerly awaited by the children
whose names are on the cover. This is *their* magazine! Their very
own! This feeling of pride and ownership is another added stimula-
tion to open the covers right away and to begin reading. It is an
effective way to make readers of children.

When we looked through the large number of magazines that
had arrived from all over the world, we found not only an enormous
variety of design, format, emphasis, and mission, but an even greater
variety of editorial approaches for engaging young readers. There
were many excellent photographic nature essays for different age
groups, often beautifully illustrated fiction and nonfiction stories,
poetry, songs, many humorous selections, even quality comics.
Unfortunately, we could only read magazines written in English,
French, and German, and so had to rely on the information con-
tained in the questionnaires about each magazine's history, mission,
and editorial focus.

It is not only difficult, but also dangerous to make generaliza-
tions about magazines you cannot read. But often pictures and
photographs were quite eloquent, and I will venture a few general
observations.

In Iran, the USSR, and China, magazines for young adults (12-
to 16- year-olds) concentrate much more on serious science,
technology, math, and thinking skills than comparable magazines in
Western countries, including the U.S., where teen magazines seem
to be more frivolous and lightweight, discussing fashion, makeup,
and pop culture. There seems to be a greater emphasis on history,
current events, and politics in magazines from Western and Eastern
Europe than in periodicals from other countries. Many include as
part of their mission a desire to break down prejudice and encourage
open-mindedness. Revolutions and wars, especially World War II,
had far-reaching effects on the development of children's magazines, often changing ownership, editorial mission, and therefore
content. After World War II, many periodicals, especially in
Europe, were flooded with comics mostly from America. Literary
magazines that had flourished in these countries around the turn of
the century ceased publication with the advent of these new strip
features.

The history and development of children's magazines in any
country becomes an important issue in that country's history of
children's literature -- as important as the development of children's

book publishing. Many young authors and illustrators regard their work for children's magazines as an inseparable part of their creative development, and many already established authors and artists welcome periodicals as a way to showcase their work for thousands and often millions of young readers. However, especially considering the importance of the genre, there has been disappointingly little research done on historical, comparative, or critical issues in the field of children's periodicals. It is my hope that this exhibit will stimulate scholars and critics to direct their attention to this vast and neglected area.

I want to take this opportunity to thank the members of my committee for their help: Ron McCutchan, Art Director, *Cricket* magazine; Carolyn Yoder, Editor-in-Chief, *Cobblestone* magazine; Selma K. Richardson, Jeffrey Garrett, and Dr. James Fraser. For invaluable help in finding names of magazines and children's literature experts around the world, I especially thank Dr. Bode, Leoba Betten, Evelyn Hohne, Christa Stegemann, Werner Küffner, Doris Pfeiffer, Jelle van Ham, Gerlinde Burger, Fumiko Ganzenmüller--all of the International Youth Library, Munich; Dr. Lucia Binder of the International Institute for Children's Literature and Reading Research in Vienna; and Barbara Scharioth of the Arbeitskreis für Jugendliteratur, Munich. Thanks go also to the *Cricket* editors, John Toraason, Designer, and especially to Julie Peterson, Editorial Assistant, who organized, typed, and filed a huge amount of correspondence and finally entered the information from the 271 questionnaires into the computer, together with Natalie Publow, Editorial Intern.

Marianne Carus

Marianne Carus
Publisher and Editor-in-Chief
Cricket

EUROPE

Fatosi

Publisher: Komiteti Qëndror i BRPSH
Bulevardi Stalin
Tiranë
Albania

For ages 6 to 10; typical reader is 9
24 issues per year
25,000 copies sold per issue
Format: 24 pages; black and color; 18 x 26 cm; stapled
Editor-in-Chief: Xhevat Beqaraj
Art Director: Alida Frashëri
Editorial mission: the moral and political education of children
Editorial content: literature, nature, science, history, education, art, sports, crafts, comics, puzzles, riddles; children's contributions and letters

Founded in 1959 by Bedri Dedja as a monthly, *Fatosi* became a semimonthly in 1970. It is government owned. A little boy, the mascot, symbolizes the reader of the magazine.

Klex (Blotch)

Publisher: Kinderzeitung-Zeitschriften &
Verlagsgesellschaft, m.b.H
Marc-Aurel-Strasse 10-12
A-1010 Vienna
Austria

For ages 8 to 14
20 issues per year
150,000 copies sold per issue
Format: 16 pages; black and white/full color section;
21 x 30 cm; unbound
Editor-in-Chief: Peter Michael Lingens
Editorial mission: to make information about politics, economics,
and culture easily accessible to children
Editorial content: literature, science, education, music, sports,
comics, crafts, puzzles, politics, economics, culture; children's
contributions and letters

Peter Michael Lingens founded *Klex* magazine in 1987 based on the
French *Journal des Enfants* (Children's Newspaper).

Topic

Publisher: Kinderzeitung Zeitschriften-
Verlagsgesellschaft m.b.H.
Am Modenapark 6/9
A-1030 Vienna
Austria

For ages 11 to 16
20 issues per year
180,000 copies sold per issue
Format: 16 pages; black and white/full color pages; 21
x 28.5 cm; glued
Editor-in-Chief: Peter Michael Lingens
Art Director: Robert Dempfer
Editorial mission: to provide material about politics,
economy, social and cultural affairs, sports, science, and
environmental pollution
Editorial content: nature, science, history, education,
astronomy, art, music, social science, sports, crafts,
puzzles; readers' contributions and letters

Topic was started by Peter Michael Lingens in 1987. It
is to become a full color monthly in September 1990.

Weite Welt (Wide World)

Publisher: Missionshaus St. Gabriel
A-2340 Mödling
Austria

For ages 8 to 14
11 issues per year
60,000 copies sold per issue
Format: 28 pages; black and white/full color section;
20 x 28 cm; stapled
Editor-in-Chief: Ingrid Weixelbaumer
Art Director: Piotr Stolarczyk
Editorial mission: to provide children with entertainment, information, and religion
Editorial content: religion, animals, foreign countries,
comics, crafts; children's contributions and letters

Weite Welt was founded in 1920 as *Jesus-Knabe* by the
Divine Word Missionary Brothers. The magazine's
name changed to *Weite Welt* in 1966. It is a church
publication and has a little elephant as a mascot.

Kartinna Galerija (Art Gallery)

Publisher: Union of Bulgarian Writers and Union of Bulgarian
Painters
Plostad Slavejkov 2-A
1000 Sofia
Bulgaria

For ages 10 to 14
10 issues per year
13,000 copies sold per issue
Format: 16 pages; black and color; 20 x 28 cm; stapled
Editor-in-Chief: Rosen Vasilev
Art Director: Peter Petrov
Editorial mission: to broaden children's knowledge of art and
literature
Editorial content: literature, art; children's contributions and letters

Kartinna Galerija was founded in 1925 by Georgi Palashev. The
Russian version of the magazine has 31,000 subscribers and may be
purchased in the USSR.

Slaveiche

Anguel Kunchev 5
1000 Sofia
Bulgaria

For ages 3 to 8
10 issues per year
110,500 copies sold per issue
Format: 16 pages; full color; 26.5 x 19.5 cm; stapled
Editor-in-Chief: Gueorgi Stroumski
Art Director: Nikolay Stoyanov
Editorial mission: to enrich children's intellectual lives with
literature and art
Editorial content: literature, skill-developing games

Although the first issues of *Slaveiche* were published in the early
1900's, it was not issued regularly until 1957, under the leadership
of Luchesar Stanchev. Petko R. Slaveykov, a prominent Bulgarian
poet, is considered to be the magazine's father.

ABC Mladych Techniku a Príodovedcu
(ABC of Young Technicians and Natural Scientists)

Publisher: Mladá Fronta
PNS, Jindrisská 14
Prague 1, 110 00
Czechoslovakia

For ages 10 to 15
24 issues per year
310,000 copies sold per issue
Format: 48 pages; full color; 21 x 28.5 cm; perfect-bound
Editor-in-Chief: Vlastislav Toman
Art Directors: Zd. Kocourková, I. Holicová
Editorial content: literature, fantasy, nature, science, history,
science fiction, astronomy, anthropology, crafts, comics, technical
features; children's contributions and letters

Founded by CSM in 1957 as a 32-page monthly, this youth
organization magazine has grown to be a full color 48-page
semimonthly today.

Materidouska (Thyme)

Publisher: Mladá Fronta
Artia Ve Smeckách 30
11127 Prague 1
Czechoslovakia

For ages 6 to 8
12 issues per year
330,000 copies sold per issue
Format: 32 pages; full color; 16.5 x 24 cm; stapled
Editor-in-Chief: Jirina Cerníková
Art Director: Jan Zbánek
Editorial mission: literary and aesthetic education
Editorial content: literature, fables, art, puzzles; children's contributions and letters

Founded in 1945 by the Czech poet Frantisek Hrubín, the magazine has grown from 16 to 32 pages.

Ohnícek (Bonfire)

Publisher: Mladá Fronta
Radlická 61
15002 Prague 5
Czechoslovakia

For ages 8 to 11
24 issues per year
270,000 copies sold per issue
Format: 32 pages; black and white/full color sections; 24 x 16.5 cm; stapled
Editor-in-Chief: Eva Vondrásková
Art Director: Vera Faltová
Editorial mission: to educate and teach moral values
Editorial content: literature, fantasy, nature, science, history, science fiction, education, art, music, social science, sports, crafts, comics, puzzles, world news; children's contributions and letters

Ohnícek was founded in 1950 by the Mladá Fronta publishing house. Its mascot is the dog Barbáner.

Pionyr (Pioneer)

Publisher: Mladá Fronta
Radlická 61
150 02 Prague 5
Czechoslovakia

For ages 12 to 16
12 issues per year
135,000 copies sold per issue
Format: 48 pages; full color; 20.5 x 22.5 cm; stapled
Editor-in-Chief: Vladimír Klevis
Art Director: Jirí Votruba
Editorial mission: to educate readers in the arts, literature, and history
Editorial content: literature, fantasy, history, education, art, music, social science, crafts, interviews with artists, entertainment; children's contributions and letters

Pionyr is a government-owned publication founded in 1953 by the Mladá Fronta publishing house.

Slunicko

Publisher: Mladá Fronta
Artia, Ve Smeckách 30
11127 Prague 1
Czechoslovakia

For children under 6
12 issues per year
300,000 copies sold per issue
Format: 32 pages; full color; 19.3 x 24 cm; stapled
Editor-in-Chief: Jan Kruta
Art Director: Jan Pacák
Editorial mission: to introduce preschoolers to the
world around them and to be their first "magazine-toy"
Editorial content: literature, education, music, sports,
crafts, comics; children's contributions and letters

Slunicko was founded in 1967 by Jan Kloboucník and
the Mladá Fronta publishing house.

Stezka

Publisher: Mladá Fronta
PNS, Jindrìsská 14
Prague 1,   110 00
Czechoslovakia

For ages 10 to 15
12 issues per year
Format: 48 pages; full color; 22.5 x 29.5 cm; perfect-
bound
Editor-in-Chief: Jirì Prchal
Art Director: Stanislava Jelínková
Editorial content: literature, fantasy, nature, science,
history, sports, crafts, comics, tourism; children's
contributions and letters

Stezka was founded in 1969 by Mladá Fronta and CSM.

Kamarát (Friend)

Publisher: Smena
Prazská 11
812 84 Bratislava
Czechoslovakia

For ages 11 to 15
52 issues per year
130,000 copies sold per issue
Format: 16 pages; black and white/full color section;
26.5 x 31.5 cm; stapled
Editor-in-Chief: Andrej Holan
Art Directors: Pavol Moravcík, Ivan Hojny
Editorial mission: to be a friend, helper, and adviser to
children
Editorial content: general interest including special
features such as Doctor's Advice and the Confidence
Line; children's contributions and letters

Kamarát was founded in 1968 by the children's organization SUR PO CSM. Its precursor was Pionierske
Noviny (The Pioneers' Gazette), a weekly founded in
1949.

Ohník (The Little Fire)

Publisher: Smena
Karpatská 2
812 84 Bratislava
Czechoslovakia

For ages 9 to 11
24 issues per year
243,000 copies sold per issue
Format: 16 pages; full color; 20 x 29 cm; stapled
Editor-in-Chief: Magdaléna Gocníková
Art Director: Tatjana Kramárová
Editorial mission: to entertain
Editorial content: general interest, sports, activities,
children's inventions; children's contributions and
letters

Ohník was founded in 1948 by the Slovak Pedagogical
Publishing House. It is owned by the government and
has two mascots: a boy named Ohník and a girl named
Ohnícka.

Vcielka (Little Honey Bee)

Publisher: Smena
Dostojevského rad 1
812 84 Bratislava
Czechoslovakia

For ages 3 to 6
24 issues per year
125,000 copies sold per issue
Format: 16 pages; full color; 21 x 14.8 cm; perfect-bound
Editor-in-Chief: Dana Guricanová
Art Director: Hana Krepopová
Editorial mission: to educate and amuse preschool children and to develop their aesthetic sense, logical thinking, and motor coordination
Editorial content: general interest; children's contributions

Founded by the Slovak General Committee of the Czechoslovak Union of Youth in 1959, *Vcielka* is a government-owned publication of the SUV SZM/ Socialist Union of Youth. The magazine's mascot is a honeybee named Meduska.

Zornicka

Publisher: Smena
Gottwaldovo nám.6
813 81 Bratislava
Czechoslovakia

For ages 7 to 9
24 issues per year
164,000 copies sold per issue
Format: 16 pages; full color; 20 x 29 cm; stapled
Editor-in-Chief: Peter Stilicha
Art Director: Natasa Mojzisová
Editorial mission: to provide good material for young readers
Editorial content: literature, comics, puzzles; children's contributions and letters

Zornicka was founded in 1948 by the Slovenské Pedagogické Nakladatel'stvo publishing house in Bratislava, as a monthly for young readers.

Slniecko (Little Sun)

Publisher: Mladé Letá
Suvorovova 3
815 19 Bratislava
Czechoslovakia

For ages 7 to 12
10 issues per year
38,653 copies sold per issue
Format: 32 pages; full color; 21 x 26.5 cm; stapled
Editor-in-Chief: Ján Turan
Art Directors: Ondrej Máriássy, Marián Skripek
Editorial mission: to promote ethnic and aesthetic sensibilities in children and to encourage their appreciation of national history
Editorial content: literature, history, art, interviews with artists, serials; children's contributions and letters

Founded in 1927 by Rudolf Klacko, *Slniecko* was published by the Matica Slovenská publishing house in Martin until 1950. It is now owned by the government. Its symbol is called Little Sun.

EUROPE

DENMARK

Krible Krable

Publisher: Arnis aps
Postboks 130, Toendervej 197
DK-6200 Aabenraa
Denmark

For ages 9 to 13
3 issues per year
Format: 56 pages; black and white; 17.5 x 24.5 cm; stapled
Editor-in-Chief: Jakob Gormsen
Editorial mission: to cultivate in readers a love for reading and fine art
Editorial content: literature, fantasy, art; children's contributions

Krible Krable was first published in 1989 by Jakob Gormsen and Finn Barlby. It was inspired by the American literary magazine for children, *Cricket*. Its name is taken from a well-known tale by Hans Christian Andersen.

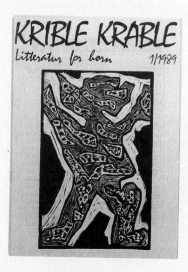

Frösi

Publisher: Verlag Junge Welt
Mauerstrasse 39140
1080 Berlin
East Germany

For ages 9 to 13
12 issues per year
Format: 32 to 40 pages; black and color/full color pages; 23.75 x
28.5 cm; stapled
Editor-in-Chief: Wilfried Weidner
Art Director: Vera Kruse
Editorial mission: to entertain
Editorial content: literature, fantasy, nature, science, history,
education, art, music, anthropology, sports, craft insert, comics,
puzzles; children's contributions and letters

Frösi was founded in 1953.

EUROPE

EAST
GERMANY

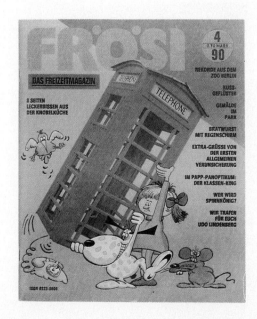

Benni

Publisher: Weltbild Verlag
Frauentorstr. 5
8900 Augsburg
West Germany

For ages 6 to 10
12 issues per year
Format: 28 pages; full color; 21.5 x 27 cm; stapled
Editor-in-Chief: Marilis Lunkenbein
Art Director: Robert Erker
Editorial content: literature, nature, education, religion, sports, crafts, comics, puzzles; children's contributions and letters

Benni was founded in 1984 by the Weltbild Verlag. It is a church publication. Its mascot is the character Benni.

Bimbo

Publisher: Johann-Michael-Sailer-Verlag
Ausserer Laufer Platz 22
18500 Nürnberg 1
West Germany

For ages 6 to 10
12 issues per year
130,000 copies sold per issue
Format: 20 pages; full color; 19 x 25.5 cm; stapled
Editor-in-Chief: Stefan Rümmele
Art Director: Hans-Peter Schellhorn
Editorial mission: to teach children about animals
and nature
Editorial content: nature, crossword puzzles, quizzes,
posters; children's contributions and letters

Bimbo was begun by Wilfred Beuerle in 1977. Bimbo
the elephant is its mascot.

Stafette (Horse Messenger)

Publisher: Johann-Michael-Sailer-Verlag
Ausserer Laufer Platz 22
D-8500 Nürnberg 1
West Germany

For ages 10 to 16
12 issues per year
Format: 48 pages; full color; 21 x 27 cm; stapled
Editor-in-Chief: Eduard W. Länger
Editorial content: general interest; children's
contributions and letters

Stafette was founded in 1946 by
Sebaldus-Verlag, Nürnberg.

Tierfreund (Animal Friend)

Publisher: Johann-Michael-Sailer-Verlag
Ausserer Laufer Platz 22
8500 Nürnberg 1
West Germany

For ages 10 to 15; typical reader is a high school student
12 issues per year
160,000 copies sold per issue
Format: 48 pages; full color; 21.5 x 27 cm; stapled
Editor-in-Chief: Stefan Rümmele
Art Directors: Inge Kolbe, Hans-Peter Schellhorn
Editorial mission: to teach young people about animals, plants, rural themes, and nature in general
Editorial content: nature, puzzles; children's contributions and letters

Founded in 1949 by Theodora Rosenberg and Rudolf Kumans, *Tierfreund* is sold today in Switzerland and Austria, as well as in West Germany.

Der Bunte Hund
(The Motley Dog)

Publisher: Beltz & Gelberg
Postfach 1120
6940 Weinheim
West Germany

For ages 7 to 13
3 issues per year
3,000 copies sold per issue
Format: 64 pages; full color; 21 x 27.4 cm; stapled
Editor-in-Chief: Hans-Joachim Gelberg
Art Director: Hans-Joachim Gelberg
Editorial mission: to introduce literature and art in all of its many
forms, varieties, and possibilities; to discover important new artists
and authors
Editorial content: literature; children's contributions including
literary criticism and letters

The concept for *Der Bunte Hund* was developed in 1981 by publisher Hans-Joachim Gelberg, his daughter Barbara, and children's
authors Achim Bröger and Christine Nöstlinger. There is no
comparable magazine for children in West Germany.

Floh (Flea)

Publisher: Domino Verlag
Hubertusstr. 22
8000 München 19
West Germany

For ages 10 to 15
26 issues per year
Format: 32 pages; black and white/full color sections; 21 x 29.5 cm; stapled
Editor-in-Chief: Stefan Ludwig
Editorial mission: to promote reading, provide information, and entertain
Editorial content: nature, science, history, science fiction, astronomy, art, music, anthropology, sports, crafts, comics, puzzles; children's letters

Floh is the oldest existing German youth magazine. Like *Flohkiste*, *Floh* developed from *Jugendlust*, which was founded in 1875. Its mascot is a flea named Floh.

Flohkiste (Fleabag)
Grade 1

Publisher: Domino Verlag
Hubertusstr. 22
8000 München 19
West Germany

For ages 6 and 7
26 issues per year
Format: 24 pages; black and white/full color section; 21 x 29.5 cm; stapled
Editor-in-Chief: Günther Brinek
Editorial mission: to promote reading, to provide educational material written in a style different from that of textbooks, and to entertain
Editorial content: nature, science, history, anthropology, sports, crafts, comics, puzzles, original stories; children's letters

The oldest existing German children's magazine, *Flohkiste* was founded by the Bavarian Teachers' Association in 1875 under the name *Jugendlust.* Its mascot is Flokiste, a flea.

Flohkiste (Fleabag)
Grades 2 and 3

Publisher: Domino Verlag
Hubertusstr. 22
8000 München 19
West Germany

For ages 7 to 9
26 issues per year
Format: 28 pages; black and white/full color section; 21 x 29.5 cm; stapled
Editor-in-Chief: Günther Brinek
Editorial mission: to promote reading, to provide educational material written in a style different from that of textbooks, and to entertain
Editorial content: nature, science, history, anthropology, sports, crafts, comics, puzzles, original stories; children's letters

This magazine is a sister publication to *Flohkiste* (Grade 1) and *Floh.* Since 1979, each of these has been designed for use in a specific school grade or grades.

G-Geschichte mit Pfiff
(History with Pizazz)

Publisher: J.M. Sailer Verlag GmbH
Aüsserer Laufer Platz 22
D-8500 Nürnberg 1
West Germany

For ages 10 and up
12 issues per year
32,000 copies sold per issue
Format: 52 pages; full color/black and white; 21 x 28 cm; stapled
Editor-in-Chief: Franz Metzger
Art Director: Hans-Peter Schellhorn
Editorial mission: to present the history of mankind from the Stone Age to the present
Editorial content: history

Founded as a students' general history magazine in 1979, *G-Geschichte mit Pfiff* appeals to all ages. It is popular in schools, but over 50% of its readers are adults.

Hoppla (Oops)

Publisher: Weltbild Verlag GmbH
Frauentorstrasse 5, Postfach 100085
8900 Augsburg
West Germany

For ages 3 to 7
12 issues per year
6,000 copies sold per issue
Format: 44 pages; full color; 20.5 x 23.5 cm; stapled
Editor-in-Chief: Marilis Kurz
Art Director: Robert Erker
Editorial mission: to provide educational and entertaining material
which preschoolers and parents can enjoy together
Editorial content: fantasy, nature, religion, stories, games,
activities, parents' guide

Hoppla is a licensed edition of the French children's magazine
Pomme d'Api. It was founded by Günter A. Schmid of Weltbild
Verlag and Bayard Presse of Paris in 1989.

Junge Zeit (Youths' Time)

Publisher: Junge Zeit-Verlag
Frauentorstr. 5
D-8900 Augsburg
West Germany

For ages 14 to 20
12 issues per year
60,000 copies sold per issue
Format: 60 pages; black and white/full color sections;
21 x 28 cm; stapled
Editor-in-Chief: Rosina Wälischmiller
Art Directors: Robert Erker, Elisabeth Klingenberg
Editorial mission: to offer readers a Christian philosophy of life
Editorial content: literature, nature, education, music, religion, social science, sports, comics, puzzles, news, advice, pen pals; readers' poems and letters

Junge Zeit is a church publication, founded by Bavarian bishops in 1972.

Mücke (Bug)

Publisher: Universum Verlagsanstalt
Rösslerstr. 7
6200 Wiesbaden
West Germany

For ages 8 to 11
12 issues per year
Format: 32 pages; black and color/full color sections;
21 x 28 cm; stapled
Editor-in-Chief: Sonja Student
Art Director: Hildegard Müller
Editorial mission: to provide children with a
varied-theme magazine
Editorial content: literature, crafts, games, crosswords,
nature, science; children's contributions and letters

Mücke was started by Wilhelm Oh in 1960. Its mascot
is an insect.

Mücki (Little Bug)

Publisher: Universum Verlagsanstalt
Rösslerstr. 7
6200 Wiesbaden
West Germany

For ages 6 to 8
12 issues per year
Format: 24 pages; black and color/full color sections;
21 x 28 cm; stapled
Editor-in-Chief: Sonja Student
Art Director: Hildegard Müller
Editorial mission: to provide children with a magazine
having many themes
Editorial content: literature, crafts, games, crosswords,
nature, science; children's contributions and letters

Mücki was founded by Wilhelm Oh in 1987. Its mascot
is an insect.

Teddy

Publisher: Verlag J.F. Schreiber GmbH
Postfach 285
7300 Esslingen
West Germany

For ages 6 to 11
12 issues per year
32,000 copies sold per issue
Format: 32 pages; full color; 11.2 x 22.4 cm; stapled
Editors: Walter Mahringer, Rolf Bianchi
Editorial mission: to educate, encourage reading, and entertain
Editorial content: education; children's contributions and letters

Teddy was started in 1949 by Gerhard Schreiber and Peter Recht. Its mascot is a teddy bear.

Eos

Publisher: Finlands Svenska Nykterhetsförbund
Fredsgatan 8 B
65120 Vasa
Finland

For ages 7 to 13; typical reader is a 10-year-old girl
9 issues per year
11,000 copies sold per issue
Format: 36 pages; black and color; 20.5 x 26 cm; stapled
Editor-in-Chief: Maria Holmström
Editorial mission: to give young people information about the
dangers of drugs and to suggest meaningful ways to use spare time
Editorial content: general interest, jokes, pen pals, comic strips;
children's contributions and letters

Alli Trygg-Helenius founded *Eos* in 1893. Its forerunner was a
magazine of the same name which was founded in 1854 by the
author Zakarias Topelius.

JP

Publisher: Poikien Keskus r.y.
SF-76280
Partaharju
Finland

For ages 10 to 14; typical reader is an 11-year-old boy
10 issues per year
35,150 copies sold per issue
Format: 56 pages; full color; 21 x 29.5 cm; stapled
Editor-in-Chief: Yrjö Tolvanen
Editorial mission: to help children grow in knowledge and skill
and to give them a broad view of the world
Editorial content: crafts, puzzles, doctor's column; children's
contributions and letters

JP started publication in 1938 as a boys' magazine named *Joka Poika*. Today it is written for both boys and girls and is funded by the Christian Youth Association. The magazine's mascot is a squirrel.

Koululainen

Publisher: Yhtyneet Kuvalehdet Oy
Postilokero 150
00101 Helsinki
Finland

For ages 7 to 15; typical reader is a 9- to 13-year-old girl
17 issues per year
63,000 copies sold per issue
Format: 48 pages; full color; 21.5 x 28 cm; stapled
Editor-in-Chief: Anneli Ruokonen
Art Director: Johanna Hellman
Editorial mission: to bring children joy, entertainment, and
knowledge and to encourage good manners
Editorial content: general interest; children's contributions and
letters

Koululainen was founded in 1944 by the Association of the Elementary School Teachers. The magazine had a very difficult beginning but later gained a faithful readership. Its mascot is a parrot named Taavi.

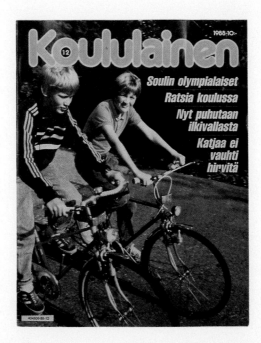

Leppis (Ladybug)

Publisher: Lasten Keskus Oy
Särkiniementie 7 A
00210 Helsinki
Finland

For ages 4 to 9
8 issues per year
6,000 copies sold per issue
Format: 32 pages; full color; 17.5 x 25 cm; stapled
Editors: Pertti Luumi, Marja-Leena Toivanen
Art Director: Sini Pellonpää
Editorial mission: to make a good and jolly magazine for children
Editorial content: literature, crafts, nature, comics, Bible stories;
children's contributions and letters

Leppäkerttu, the forerunner of *Leppis*, was founded in 1981 by
Lasten Keskus. *Leppis* started publication in 1987. Its mascot
is a ladybug.

Nuorten Sarka

Publisher: Suomen 4H-liitto
Bulevardi 28
00120 Helsinki
Finland

For ages 8 to 17; typical reader is a 4H Club member
10 issues per year
31,000 copies sold per issue
Format: 40 pages; full color; 21 x 29.5 cm; stapled
Editor-in-Chief: Pentti Lindsberg
Editorial mission: to educate
Editorial content: nature, science, education, music, crafts,
puzzles; children's contributions and letters

Founded in 1945, *Nuorten Sarka* is a nonprofit publication closely
associated with 4H Club.

Syppi

Publisher: Union Bank of Finland
Pl 70
00101 Helsinki
Finland

For ages 7 to 14
6 issues per year
Format: 32 pages per issue; full color; 23 x 27 cm; stapled
Editor-in-Chief: Marja Männistö
Editorial content: general interest, nature, economy, hobbies;
children's contributions and letters

Syppi, a nonprofit publication, was founded by the Union Bank of
Finland in 1977.

Abricot (Apricot)

Publisher: Les Publications du Labyrinthe
2, Rue Villa Franca
75015 Paris
France

For ages 18 months to 4 years
12 issues per year
50,000 copies sold per issue
Format: 32 pages; full color; 19.5 x 20 cm; stapled
Editor-in-Chief: Marc Eskenazi
Art Director: Anita Fizet
Editorial mission: to provide toddlers with their first magazine and
to give parents an opportunity to be close to their toddlers
Editorial content: general interest, original stories and illustrations

Abricot was started by Marc Eskenazi in 1987. A little girl, Mila, is
its mascot.

Astrapi

Publisher: Bayard Presse
3 Rue Bayard
Paris 75008
France

For ages 7 to 11; typical reader is 9
24 issues per year
95,000 copies sold per issue
Format: 32 pages; full color; 21 x 28.5 cm; stapled
Editor-in-Chief: Catherine Peugeot
Art Director: Claude Delafosse
Editorial mission: to educate and entertain
Editorial content: general interest; children's letters

Astrapi was founded in 1978 by Anne-Marie de Besombes and Jacqueline Kerguéno. At the request of parents and children, the magazine has recently started publishing more nonfiction. Touffin, a dog, is the magazine's mascot.

Images Doc

Publisher: Bayard Presse
3 Rue Bayard
75008 Paris
France

For ages 8 to 12
12 issues per year
100,000 copies sold per issue
Format: 65 pages; full color; 19 x 19.5 cm; perfect-bound
Editor-in-Chief: Françoise Récamier
Art Director: Pascale Guyon
Editorial mission: to help children discover and learn about the world—present, past, and future—through pictures
Editorial content: general interest, nonfiction, original photographs and illustrations

Images Doc was founded in 1989 by Françoise Récamier and Anne-Marie de Besombes as a response to schoolchildren's interest in more nonfiction articles and pictures. Children collect the pictures and use the magazine to help with schoolwork.

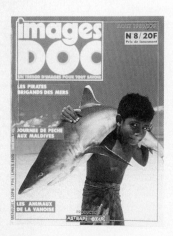

Je Bouquine (I Read)

Publisher: Bayard Presse
3, Rue Bayard
75008 Paris
France

For ages 10 to 14
12 issues per year
65,000 copies sold per issue
Format: 108 pages; full color; 18 x 24.5 cm; perfect-bound
Editors: Béatrice Valentin, Anne-Marie de Besombes
Art Director: Isabelle Fuhrman
Editorial mission: to encourage children to read
Editorial content: literature, comics, book and film reviews; children's contributions and letters

Je Bouquine was founded by Bayard Presse in 1984.

Okapi

Publisher: Bayard Presse
3 Rue Bayard
75393 Paris Cedex 08
France

For ages 10 to 15
24 issues per year
105,000 copies sold per issue
Format: 56 pages; full color; 20.5 x 28.2 cm; stapled
Editorial Director: Anne-Marie De Besombes
Art Director: Patrick Couratin
Editorial mission: to enable readers to discover and learn about French culture
Editorial content: geography, history, science, news, true stories, fiction, comics, religion, art, music, sports, crafts, puzzles; children's letters

Okapi was founded by Yves Beccaria in 1971 for readers from 7 to 12 years of age. Since 1978, it has been directed at readers aged 10 to 15, both in France and French-speaking countries around the world.

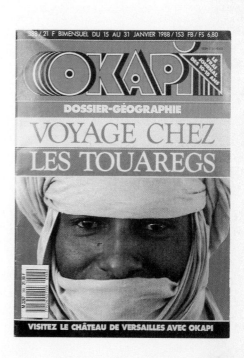

Les Belles Histoires (Beautiful Stories)

Publisher: Bayard Presse
3 Rue Bayard
75008 Paris
France

For ages 3 to 7
12 issues per year
80,000 copies sold per issue
Format: 48 pages; full color; 20.5 x 23.5 cm; stapled
Editor-in-Chief: Marie-Hélène Delval
Art Director: Michèle Isvy
Editorial mission: to publish quality original stories and illustrations
Editorial content: original stories and illustrations

Les Belles Histoires was founded in 1972 by Bayard Presse.

J'Aime Lire (I Love to Read)

Publisher: Bayard Presse
3 Rue Bayard
75008 Paris
France

For ages 7 to 10
12 issues per year
255,000 copies sold per issue
Format: 68 pages; full color; 15.5 x 19 cm; perfect-bound
Editor-in-Chief: Jacqueline Kerguéno
Art Director: Martin Berthommier
Editorial mission: to encourage beginning readers
Editorial content: literature, comics; children's contributions

J'Aime Lire was founded in 1977 by Jacqueline Kerguéno and Anne-Marie de Besombes. It is published in many languages and has three mascots: Bonnemine (a little pencil), Tom-Tom (a little boy), and his sister Nana.

Pomme D'Api (Small Apple)

Publisher: Bayard Presse
3 Rue Bayard
75008 Paris
France

For ages 3 to 7
12 issues per year
160,000 copies sold per issue
Format: 40 pages; full color; 20.5 x 23.5 cm; stapled
Editor-in-Chief: Marie-Hèlène Delval
Art Director: Michèle Isvy
Editorial mission: to help children develop
intellectually, artistically, and spiritually
Editorial content: stories, games, cartoons, parents'
section

Pomme D'Api was started in 1966 by Bayard Presse, as
the first French magazine for children under 7 years of
age. Its mascots are Ti-Michou, a little boy, his dog, and
a little brown bear.

Popi

Publisher: Bayard Presse
3 Rue Bayard
75008 Paris
France

For ages 18 months to 3 years
12 issues per year
95,000 copies sold per issue
Format: 22 pages; full color; 19 x 20 cm; stapled
Editor-in-Chief: Marie-Hèlène Delval
Art Director: Michèle Isvy
Editorial mission: to help young children develop
visual and language skills
Editorial content: stories, pictures, games

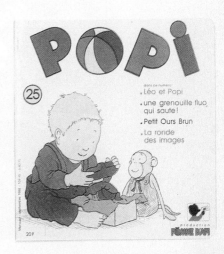

Popi was started in 1986 by Bayard Presse in response
to the new parental concern about early childhood
development. Leo, a little boy, and his toy monkey,
Popi, are characters that appear every month.

Youpi (Yippee)

Publisher: Bayard Presse
3 et 5 Rue Bayard
75008 Paris
France

For ages 3 to 6; typical reader is a 5-year-old boy
12 issues per year
Format: 36 pages; full color; 23 x 26 cm; stapled
Editor-in-Chief: Mijo Beccaria
Art Director: Thierry Courtin
Editorial mission: to develop young childen's autonomy and
knowledge of the world around them
Editorial content: general interest, games, documentaries

Youpi was founded in 1988 by Mijo Beccaria. The magazine's
mascot is Youpi, a kangaroo.

Diabolo

Publisher: Milan Editions
300 Rue Léon Joulin
31101 Toulouse Cedex 100
France

For ages 7 to 9
12 issues per year
Format: 48 pages; full color; 21 x 27 cm; stapled
Editor-in-Chief: Patrice Amen
Art Director: Gilbert Noguès
Editorial mission: to educate
Editorial content: literature, nature, science, history, education, sports, games, photographs, activities

Diabolo was founded by Patrice Amen and Alain Oriol in 1987.

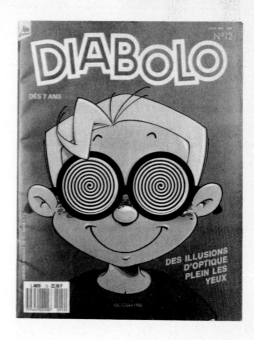

Toboggan

Publisher: Editions Milan
300 Rue Léon Joulin
31101 Toulouse Cedex 100
France

For ages 4 to 6
12 issues per year
Format: 40 pages; full color; 22 x 24 cm; stapled
Editor-in-Chief: Patrice Amen
Art Director: Gilbert Noguès
Editorial mission: to educate
Editorial content: literature, nature, education, games, comics, parents' pages; children's letters

Toboggan was founded in 1980 by Patrice Amen and Alain Oriol. Jules and Zoé Mimosa are two of the magazine's regular fictional characters.

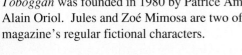

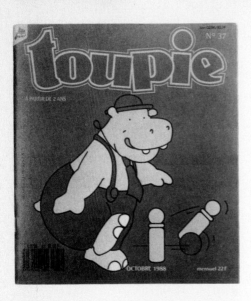

Toupie (Spinning Top)

Publisher: Editions Milan
300 Rue Léon Joulin
31101 Toulouse Cedex 100
France

For ages 2 to 4
12 issues per year
Format: 40 pages; full color; 21 x 23.5 cm; stapled
Editor-in-Chief: Patrice Amen
Art Director: Gilbert Noguès
Editorial mission: to educate
Editorial content: nature, education, crafts, comics

Toupie was founded by Patrice Amen and Alain Oriol in 1985. Coline, Colas, and Mousse are characters that appear every month.

Wapiti

Publisher: Editions Milan
300 Rue Léon Joulin
31101 Toulouse Cedex 100
France

For ages 7 to 12
12 issues per year
Format: 48 pages; full color; 21.5 x 27 cm; perfect-bound
Editor-in-Chief: Patrice Amen
Art Director: Gilbert Noguès
Editorial mission: to educate
Editorial content: nature, science, education, sports; children's contributions and letters

Wapiti was founded in 1987 by Patrice Amen and Alain Oriol. César, a bird, is the magazine's mascot.

Mikado

Publisher: Editions Milan
300 Rue Léon Joulin
31101 Toulouse Cedex 100
France

For ages 9 to 12
12 issues per year
Format: 48 pages; full color; 22 x 27 cm; stapled
Editor-in-Chief: Patrice Amen
Art Director: Gilbert Noguès
Editorial mission: to educate
Editorial content: literature, nature, science, education, sports, crafts, games, comics, photographs; children's contributions and letters

Mikado was founded in 1983 by Patrice Amen and Alain Oriol.

Gullivore

Publisher: Francs et Franches Camarades
10.14 Rue Tolain
75020 Paris
France

60,000 copies sold per issue
Format: 64 pages; full color;
21 x 28.5 cm; stapled
Editor-in-Chief: Christian Robin
Editorial content: science, nature, sports, history, comics, puzzles, crafts

Gullivore was founded in 1987 by the publishers of *Jeunes Années*.

Jeunes Années (Young Years)

Publisher: Francs et Franches Camarades
10.14 Rue Tolain
75020 Paris
France

For ages 3 to 8
5 issues per year
100,000 copies sold per issue
Format: 32 pages; full color;
28.5 x 21.2 cm; stapled
Editor-in-Chief: Christian Robin
Art Director: Françoise Dromigny
Editorial mission: to provide children with activities
Editorial content: literature, nature, science, history, activities, comics, puzzles; children's poems and letters

Jeunes Années was founded by Fernand Bouteille in 1953 as an annual.

Je Lis Déjà (I Already Read)

Publisher: Fleurus Presse
21, Rue du Faubourg Saint Antoine
75550 Paris Cedex 11
France

For ages 5 to 7
10 issues per year
45,000 copies sold per issue
Format: 52 pages; full color; 14.8 x 19 cm;
perfect-bound
Editor-in-Chief: Béatrice Guthart
Art Director: Eliane Crocé
Editorial mission: to be the first little book a child can
read independently
Editorial content: original literature and illustrations

Je Lis Déjà was started by Béatrice Guthart in 1989.
Mic, Cola, and their bird, Blabla, are characters that
appear regularly in the magazine.

Perlin

Publisher: Fleurus Presse
21, Rue du Faubourg Saint-Antoine
75011 Paris
France

For ages 4 to 7
52 issues per year
61,350 copies sold per issue
Format: 16 pages; full color; 21 x 28 cm;
perfect-bound
Editor-in-Chief: Béatrice Guthard
Editorial content: education, religion, original stories,
comics; children's poems and letters

Perlin was started in 1952 under the name
Perlin & Piupin.

La Hulotte (Tawny Owl)

Publisher: C.P.N.C.A. Société de Protection de la La Nature
Boult-aux-Bois
F-08240 Buzancy
France

For ages 8 and up
2 issues per year
260,000 copies sold per issue
Format: 40 to 48 pages; black and white; 15 x 21 cm; stapled
Editor-in-Chief: Pierre Deom
Art Director: Pierre Deom
Editorial mission: to help children discover nature and encourage them to respect and protect it
Editorial content: the nature of France and western Europe, original stories and illustrations

La Hulotte was founded by Pierre Deom in 1972 as a nature magazine for children. Today many adults also subscribe to this nonprofit publication. La Hulotte, a tawny owl, is the mascot.

Petit Géant (Small Giant)

Publisher: Nathan-Sep Cluny
Nathan Abonnement BP 183
75665 Paris Cedex 14
France

For ages 4 to 7
11 issues per year
60,000 copies sold per issue
Format: 48 pages; full color; 22.7 x 27 cm; stapled
Editor-in-Chief: Marc Eskenazi
Art Director: Sylvia Dorance
Editorial mission: to help children learn to read
Editorial content: literature

Petit Géant was founded in 1989 by Marc Eskenazi of Nathan
publishing. Its mascots are a boy named Felix and a dog
named Klaxon.

EUROPE

GREAT
BRITAIN

Jump!

Publisher: Two-Can Publishing
27 Cowper Street
London ECZ 4AP
Great Britain (England)

For ages 4 to 8
12 issues per year
23,000 copies sold per issue
Format: 32 pages; full color; 22 x 27 cm; stapled
Editor-in-Chief: Diane James
Editorial mission: to publish a quality full color monthly magazine
Editorial content: literature, science, history, comic strip, competitions; children's contributions and letters

Jump! was founded in 1987 by Andrew Jarvis.

Owl

Publisher: The Children's Magazine Company Ltd.
Imperial Works, Perren Street
London NW5 3ED
Great Britain (England)

For ages 7 to 14
12 issues per year
40,000 copies sold per issue
Format: 32 pages; full color; 20.8 x 27.6 cm; stapled
Editors: Christopher Maynard, Graham Marks
Editorial mission: to promote interest in natural history and
environmental issues
Editorial content: nature; children's letters

Owl (UK) began publication in 1989 as a franchise of the Canadian
Owl magazine. About half of the publication's material comes from
the Canadian *Owl*.

Play and Learn

Publisher: Claiborne Publications
36 High Street
Saxmundham, Suffolk IP17 1AB
Great Britain (England)

Format: 30 pages; black and white/full color pages; 21 x 30 cm;
stapled
Editor: Michele Claiborne
Designer: Michele Claiborne
Editorial mission: to inform children about the world in an
entertaining manner
Editorial content: activities, puzzles, parent/teacher guide

Puffin Flight

Publisher: Penguin Books
27 Wright's Lane
London W85T2
Great Britain (England)

For ages 5 to 8
3 issues per year
85,000 copies sold per issue
Format: 28 pages; black and color; 21 x 29.5 cm; stapled
Editor-in-Chief: Alison Stanley
Art Director: Annie Horwood
Editorial mission: to promote the pleasure of reading in general and Puffin books in particular
Editorial content: literature, puzzles; children's contributions and letters

Puffin Flight replaced the Junior Puffin Club magazine *The Egg* in 1987, when the Puffin Club amalgamated with the School Book Club. It is based on Puffin books and can only be bought through the Puffin School Book Club. Its mascot is a fat puffin.

Meet PHYLLIS ARKLE and ALFIE the film star. Plus Poems~Puzzles~Princesses~and much more!

Puffin Post

Publisher: Penguin Books
27 Wright's Lane
London W85T2
Great Britain (England)

For ages 9 to 13
3 issues per year
85,000 copies sold per issue
Format: 28 pages; black and color; 21 x 29.5 cm; stapled
Editor-in-Chief: Alison Stanley
Editorial mission: to promote the pleasure of reading in general and Puffin books in particular
Editorial content: literature, puzzles; children's contributions and letters

Founded by Kaye Webb in 1963 as the magazine of the Puffin Club, *Puffin Post* is now available to schoolchildren through the Puffin Book Club. Its mascot is a fat puffin.

Sbondonics

Publisher: Welsh Books Council
Castell Brychan, Heol-y-Bryn
Aberystwyth, Dyfed SY23 2JB
Great Britain (Wales)

For ages 7 to 11
3 issues per year
8,000 copies sold per issue
Format: 14 pages; black and color; 21 x 27.8 cm; stapled
Editor-in-Chief: Siân Teifi
Art Director: Elgan Davies
Editorial mission: to give children information about current Welsh books and to offer books at a discount price
Editorial content: book reviews, competitions, cartoon strip, puzzles; children's contributions and letters

Written in Welsh, *Sbondonics* is a publication put out by the Welsh Book Club. The magazine was founded by Dylan Williams in 1983.

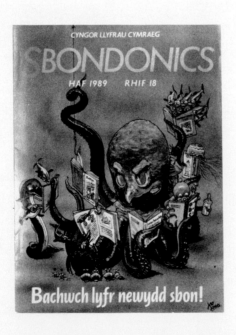

Aerostato (Balloon)

Publisher: Greek Ministry of Education
15, Metropoleos Str.
10185 Athens
Greece

For ages 8 to 13
10 issues per year
Format: 32 pages; full color; 21 x 28 cm; stapled
Editor-in-Chief: Pepi Athini
Art Director: Athina Rikaki
Editorial mission: to present entertainment and information on
Greek culture and traditions to the Greek migrants' children living in
West Germany
Editorial content: general interest; children's contributions and
letters

Aerostato is a government-owned publication founded in 1985 by
the Greek Ministry of Education. Its symbol is a balloon.

Hellenic Youth Red Cross

Publisher: Hellenic Red Cross
4, Alkiviadou Street
104 39 Athens
Greece

For ages 7 to 20
8 issues per year
20,000 copies sold per issue
Format: 32 pages; black and white; 21 x 29 cm; stapled
Editor-in-Chief: the current vice president of the Hellenic Red Cross
Editorial mission: to inform young people on all subjects that interest the Red Cross
Editorial content: literature, nature, history, education, music, religion, sports, puzzles, problems in society; children's contributions and letters

This nonprofit publication was founded by the Hellenic Red Cross in 1945. It is now funded by the same organization and often undertakes campaigns to face important national or international social problems.

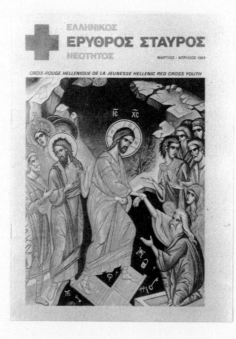

Az En Ujságom

Publisher: Móra Ferenc Publishing House
1146 Budapest
Május 1 ut 57-59
Hungary

For ages 7 to 14
5 issues per year
71,000 copies sold per issue
Format: 36 pages; black and color; 22 x 30 cm; stapled
Editor-in-Chief: Attila Csokonai
Editorial content: literature, education; children's contributions
and letters

As En Ujságom was founded by the Móra Ferenc Publishing
House in 1988.

Kincskeresö

Publisher: Ferenc Móra.
Szerkesztösége
Victor Hugo u.1
6720 Szeged
Hungary

For ages 10 to 14
9 issues per year
45,000 copies sold per issue
Format: 48 pages; black and color; 16.75 x 23.75 cm; stapled
Editor-in-Chief: Idnos Sziladi
Art Director: Katalin Tildy
Editorial mission: to provide children with cultural information and to encourage them to read
Editorial content: literature

Kincskeresö was founded in 1971 by András Uegedüs.

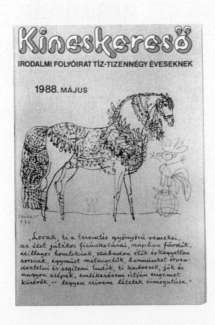

Kisdobos (Little Drummer)

Publisher: Kisdobos Szerkesztösége
Orlay u. 2/B
1117 Budapest
Hungary

For ages 6 to 10
10 issues per year
Format: 28 pages; full color; 20 x 28 cm; stapled
Editor-in-Chief: Jani Gabriella
Editorial mission: to stimulate interest in the environment and in
the wonders of nature, to popularize literature and the arts, and to
suggest useful ways to spend leisure time
Editorial content: literature, nature, science, history, activities,
puzzles; children's letters

Kisdobos was founded by the Union of Hungarian Pioneers in 1952.
The periodical's title is a reminder of the bold little drummers who
marched in the front ranks of the people's liberation struggles.

Kölyök

Publisher: Magyar Média
HELIR XIII. Lehel u. 10/a
1900 Budapest
Hungary

For ages 10 to 15; typical reader is a 13-year-old girl
11 issues per year
27,000 copies sold per issue
Format: 68 pages; black and color/full color section; 20.5 x 27.5
cm; stapled
Editor-in-Chief: Berkes Péter
Art Director: Németh Mihály
Editorial mission: to provide quality information and advice
Editorial content: general interest; children's contributions and
letters

Kölyök, a government-owned publication, was founded in 1986 by
Berkes Péter. Two children, Mibe and Bemi, have debates through-
out the magazine in every issue.

Süni

Publisher: Idegenforgalmi Propaganda Es Kado Vállalat
Angol utca 22
1149 Budapest
Hungary

For ages 8 to 14
12 issues per year
60,000 copies sold per issue
Format: 32 pages; full color; 16.3 x 22.8 cm; stapled
Editor-in-Chief: Katalin Bársony
Art Director: György Vadász
Editorial mission: to popularize natural science and to encourage
children to protect nature
Editorial content: nature, science, astronomy, anthropology,
puzzles; children's contributions and letters

Süni was founded in 1985 by OKK, TIT, Göncöl Társaság,
Budapest.

EUROPE

ICELAND

ABC

Publisher: Frjálst Framtak h/f
Armúli 18
108 Reykjavík
Iceland

For ages 6 to15
8 issues per year
9,200 copies sold per issue
Format: 64 pages; black and white/full color sections; 19.75 x 27.4 cm; stapled
Editor-in-Chief: Hildur Gísladóttir
Art Director: Guomundur Guojónsson
Editorial mission: to print entertaining and instructive materials for children
Editorial content: general interest; children's contributions and letters

ABC was founded in 1979 by Margrét Thorlasíus.

Æskan (The Youth)

Publisher: The Icelandic Grand-lodge of International
Organization of Good-Templars
Eiríksgata 5 P.O. Box 523
121 Reykjavík
Iceland

For ages 6 to 15
10 issues per year
7,740 copies sold per issue
Format: 56 pages; black and white/full color sections; 21.5 x 28
cm; stapled
Editor-in-Chief: Karl Helgason
Art Director: Offsetpjónustan Co.
Editorial mission: to promote intellectual maturity, education, and
a healthy lifestyle
Editorial content: general interest; children's contributions
and letters

Æskan was founded in 1897 by Sigurour Júl. Jóhannesson. It has
been published continuously since that time with the exception of
two years: one year there was a paper shortage and the other year a
lack of money.

Amico dei Fanciulli

Publisher: Amico dei Fanciulli
Via Porro Lambertenghi, 28
20159 Milan
Italy

For ages 6 to 12
10 issues per year
1,050 copies sold per issue
Format: 16 pages; black and color; 17 x 23 cm; stapled
Editor-in-Chief: Floriana Bleynat
Art Director: Umberto Stagnaro
Editorial mission: to support Sunday school programs
Editorial content: religion, puzzles; children's contributions and letters

Amico dei Fanciulli was founded in 1872. It is a nonprofit church publication.

European Language Institute (Various Titles)

Publisher: European Language Institute (ELI)
1989, Casella Postale 6
62019 Recanati
Italy

Format: full color; 17 x 24 cm; stapled
Editorial mission: to provide entertaining educational foreign-language material for students
Editorial content: comics, games, activities

ELI publishes specific magazines for students learning English, French, German, Spanish, Italian, Latin, and Russian. Most of these language editions are available in four levels of difficulty, designed for beginning to advanced students.

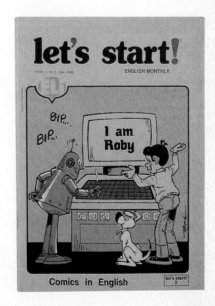

Giovani Amici

Publisher: Vitae Pensiero Ragazzi
Largo A. Gemelli 1
20123 Milan
Italy

For ages 4 to 10
12 issues per year
30,000 copies sold per issue
Format: 32 pages; full color; 21 x 28 cm; stapled
Editor-in-Chief: Roberta Maria Rosa Grazzani
Art Director: Franca Trabacchi
Editorial mission: to educate and entertain, to help children discover the pleasure of reading, and to deliver the Christian message
Editorial content: general interest, news, cartoons, stories, jokes, games; children's contributions and letters

Founded in 1934 by Padre Agostino Gemelli as a publication about the Catholic University of the Sacred Heart at Milan, *Giovani Amici* became a longer, full color, more varied magazine in 1969. Its mascots are Fiordaliso the clown and Coni the bunny rabbit.

Il Giornale dei Bambini (Children's Journal)

Publisher: Edizioni Sonda S.r.l.
Via Ciamarella, 23/3
10149 Torino
Italy

For ages 5 to 12
10 issues per year
3,300 copies sold per issue
Format: 28 pages; black and color; 22 x 34 cm; stapled
Editor-in-Chief: Antonio Monaco
Art Director: Pino Avonto
Editorial mission: to encourage young authors and artists by publishing their works
Editorial content: children's everyday experiences as reflected in their submitted poetry, diaries, stories, and art

Il Giornale dei Bambini was started in 1989. It is written and illustrated entirely by children. Parents and teachers assist the editors in collecting children's contributions. Its mascots are two children flying a kite.

Il Giornalino (The Little Journal)

Publisher: Società San Paolo Gruppo Periodici S.r.l.
Via Giotto, 36
20145 Milan
Italy

For ages 7 to 14
51 issues per year
40,000 copies sold per issue
Format: 100 pages; full color; 19.5x 26 cm; stapled
Editor-in-Chief: Tommaso Mastrandrea
Editorial mission: to educate youth and develop their creativity
Editorial content: history, sports, news, comics, entertainment; children's contributions and letters

Il Giornalino was founded in 1924 by Giacomo Alberione.

I.M. Italia Missionaria

Publisher: Pontificio Istituto Missioni Estere (P.I.M.E.)
Via Mose' Bianchi 94
20149 Milan
Italy

For ages 12 to 15; typical reader is a young religious nature-lover
10 issues per year
15,000 copies sold per issue
Format: 64 pages; full color; 17 x 24 cm; stapled
Editor-in-Chief: Giacomo Girardi
Art Director: Bruno Maggi
Editorial mission: to develop a missionary spirit in its readers
Editorial content: education, spiritual features; readers' letters

I.M. was founded by Father Paul Manna in 1919. Its mascot is Alex,
a boy who solves problems.

La Giostra
(The Merry-Go-Round)

Publisher: Anonima Veritas Editrice S.r.l.
Via Aurelia 481
Rome 00165
Italy

For ages 3 to 7; typical reader is 5
10 issues per year
63,000 copies sold per issue
Format: 32 pages; full color; 19.5 x 26.5 cm; stapled
Editor-in-Chief: Domenico Volpi
Art Director: Renato Riccioni
Editorial mission: to provide material which children and parents can enjoy together and to aid in the complete development of the child with Christian inspiration
Editorial content: literature, fantasy, nature, education, religion, crafts, comics, games, rhymes, songs, puzzles, parent/teacher guide insert; children's art

La Giostra was founded by the Azione Cattolica Italiana in 1969. Its mascots are two children, Chiara and Andrea, and five animal characters.

La Rana (The Frog)

Publisher: Touring Club Italiano
Corso Italia 10
20122 Milan
Italy

For ages 6 to 13
4 issues per year
50,000 copies sold per issue
Format: 32 pages; full color; 21 x 30 cm; stapled
Editor-in-Chief: Marialidia Minak
Art Director: Ermes Lasagni
Editorial mission: to teach young people to know and respect nature
Editorial content: nature, tourism, science, anthropology, fantasy, comics, puzzles; children's contributions and letters

La Rana was founded by Maria Marta Gilardenghi and Leonardo Idili. Its mascots are La Rana the frog and Filippo.

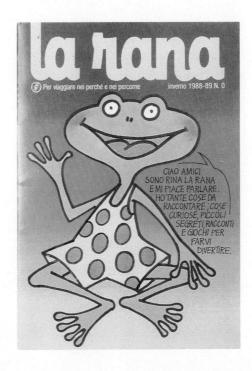

Messaggero dei Ragazzi

Publisher: Editrice Grafiche Messaggero S. Antonio
Via Orto Botanico 11
35123 Padova
Italy

For ages 9 to 16
23 issues per year
80,000 copies sold per issue
Format: 68 pages; full color; 21 x 28.5 cm; stapled
Editor-in-Chief: P. Egidio Monzani
Art Director: Giuseppe Intini
Editorial mission: to teach Christian principles and culture
Editorial content: general interest, comics; children's contributions
and letters

Messaggero dei Ragazzi was started in 1922 as a religious leaflet of
devotion to St. Anthony of Padua. It now includes cultural back-
ground as well as religious features. A computer character is its
mascot.

Panda

Publisher: The Association for World Wildlife Fund
Via Salaria, n. 290
00199 Rome
Italy

Format: 34 pages; black and color/full color pages;
21 x 27.5 cm; stapled
Editorial content: wildlife, environment, geography

Primavera Mondo Giovane

Publisher: Istituto Mazzarello
Via Laura Vicuna 1
20092 Cinisello Balsamo Milan
Italy

For ages 11 to 17
21 issues per year
150,000 copies sold per issue
Format: 80 pages; full color; 18 x 27 cm; stapled
Editor-in-Chief: Elvira Guglielmino
Art Director: Gigi Brandazza
Editorial mission: to educate young people in many ways
Editorial content: general interest; readers' contributions
and letters

Primavera Mondo Giovane was founded by Iside Malgrati in 1950
and is nonprofit.

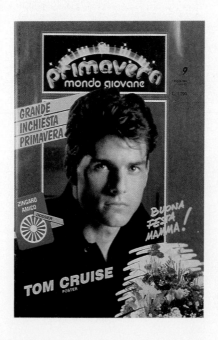

Taghna T-tfal
(Children's Own)

Publisher: Mary Puli
Malta Catholic Action, Catholic Institute
Floriana
Malta

For ages 5 to 10
9 issues per year
14,500 copies sold per issue
Format: 8 pages; black and color; 26 x 36 cm; unbound
Editor-in-Chief: Mary Puli
Art Director: Frank Vella
Editorial mission: to provide children with reading material, crafts, and a religious education
Editorial content: literature, education, religion, crafts, puzzles; children's contributions and letters

Taghna T-tfal was founded in 1980 by Mary Puli and the Malta Catholic Action. The publication is written in Maltese and is nonprofit. Authors and artists allow their work to be published free of charge and the editorial staff works for free.

Young Falcon

Publisher: Valletta Publishing
76, Old Theatre Street
Valletta
Malta

For ages 7 to 13
9 issues per year
6,000 copies sold per issue
Format: 32 pages; black and white/full color sections; 19.5 x 27.3 cm
Editor-in-Chief: Tony C. Cutajar
Editorial mission: to help children read and appreciate the English language
Editorial content: general interest; children's contributions and letters

Young Falcon was founded in 1987 by Valletta Publishing. It is the only English-language children's magazine in Malta.

Doremi

Publisher: Kok Educatief
POB 130
8260 AH Kampen
Netherlands

For ages 3 to 6
24 issues per year
Format: 16 pages; full color/black and white; 20 x 26 cm; stapled
Editor-in-Chief: Nicole Bruyr
Editorial content: fantasy; children's contributions and letters

Doremi was founded in 1955 by Patov de Kesel.

Hoj

Publisher: Kok Educatief
POB 130
8260 AH Kampen
Netherlands

For ages 6 to 8
41 issues per year
Format: 16 pages; black and color/full color pages; 20 x 26 cm; stapled
Editor-in-Chief: Nicole Pierson
Editorial content: education; children's contributions and letters

Hoj was founded in 1983.

Fryske Bernekrante

Publisher: Stichting Jacobus van Loon
Postbox 1750
8901 CB Ljouwert
Netherlands

For ages 8 to 12
10 issues per year
2,700 copies sold per issue
Format: 16 pages; black and white; 21 x 29.5 cm; stapled
Editor-in-Chief: G. Brouwer
Editorial content: literature, nature, puzzles, interviews; children's contributions and letters

Fryske Bernekrante was founded in 1981 by St. Jacobus van Loon. It is written in Frisian, a language spoken by 35,000 people in the northern region of the Netherlands.

Okki

Publisher: Malmberg b.v. Publisher
P.O. Box 233
5201 AE Den Bosch
Netherlands

For ages 7 and 8
20 issues per year
Format: 24 pages; full color/black and white; 20 x 28 cm; stapled
Editor-in-Chief: G. de Visser
Art Director: R. Spelbos
Editorial mission: to make reading enjoyable for children
Editorial content: general interest; children's letters

Okki was founded in 1919 and is distributed through the schools. Ollie Olifant, an elephant, appears in a cartoon strip in every issue.

Wie goochelt er mee? (blz. 10-11)

Taptoe

Publisher: Malmberg b.v.
P.O. Box 233
5201 AE Den Bosch
Netherlands

For ages 8 to 12
20 issues per year
Format: 24 pages; full color/black and white; 20 x 28 cm; stapled
Editor-in-Chief: G. de Visser
Art Director: I. van Woensel
Editorial mission: to make reading enjoyable for children
Editorial content: general interest; children's letters

Taptoe was founded in 1919 and is distributed through the schools. The Lotje cartoon strip appears regularly.

taptoe in de disco
Gestrikte Vaders
Het Kinderkabinet op Verkeersborden-Avontuur

Tina

Publisher: Oberon Bv
P.O. Box 6003
2001 HA Haarlem
Netherlands

For ages 9 to 15; typical reader is a 12-year-old girl
52 issues per year
105,000 copies sold per issue
Format: 40 pages; full color; 21 x 26 cm; stapled
Editor-in-Chief: Anne Marie Tassier
Art Director: Carine van Waart
Editorial mission: to provide amusement and information for girls
Editorial content: fantasy, sports, crafts, comics, children's contributions and letters

Tina was founded in 1976. The characters Tina and Debbie appear regularly in the magazine.

Stip

Publisher: Scouting Nederland
Postbus 210
3830 AE Leusden
Netherlands

For ages 7 to 10
8 issues per year
39,000 copies sold per issue
Format: 32 pages; full color/black and white; 14.5 x 21 cm; stapled
Editor-in-Chief: Trees van Mierlo
Art Director: Marijke de Groot
Editorial mission: to give children the latest scouting news and to
develop their interest in scouting skills and reading and language
abilities
Editorial content: scouting, education, general interest, comics;
children's contributions and letters

Stip was founded in 1972 by Scouting Nederland and is now funded
by the same organization. Originally it consisted solely of scouting
news, but it now contains articles and stories on various subjects. Its
mascot is a dog named Lorejas.

EUROPE

NORWAY

Norsk Barneblad

Publisher: Samyrkelaget Norsk Barneblad
Boks 524 Nanset
N-3251 Larvik
Norway

For ages 8 to 13
22 issues per year
9,000 copies sold per issue
Format: 16 to 24 pages; black and color; 20 x 26 cm; stapled
Editor-in-Chief: Olav Norheim
Editorial mission: to publish new Norwegian literature for children
Editorial content: literature, nature, science, music, comics, puzzles, pen pals, hobbies, jokes, news; children's contributions and letters

Founded in 1887 by Kristen Stalleland, *Norsk Barneblad* is the only Norwegian children's magazine independent from the influence of special organizations. Its mascots are a Norwegian blue jay and Smørbukk, a cartoon character.

Mis (Teddy Bear)

Publisher: Nasza Ksiegarnia (Our Book Store)
Spasowskiego 4
00-389 Warsaw
Poland

For ages 3 to 6; typical reader is 5
24 issues per year
600,000 copies sold per issue
Format: 20 pages; black and white/full color section;
20 x 24 cm; stapled
Editor-in-Chief: Barbara Lewandowska
Art Director: Hanna Grodzka-Nowak
Editorial mission: to introduce young readers to the fine arts and
literature in a variety of ways
Editorial content: literature, plays, picture stories, riddles, cartoons, crafts, nonfiction; children's art

Mis was founded in 1957 by Stanislaw Aleksandrzsak. In 1975 a
cartoon and cutout toy model section became a regular feature. The
difficulty of content has gradually increased.

Swiat Mlodych

Publisher: Mlodziezowa Agencja (Youth Publishing Agency)
Mokotowska 24
00-561 Warsaw
Poland

For ages 11 to 15
155 issues per year
Format: 8 pages; black and color/full color section; 30 x 41 cm;
stapled
Editor-in-Chief: Staniskaw Borowiecki
Editorial mission: to encourage extracurricular interests
Editorial content: general interest, news, children's organizations,
cartoons, humor, music, entertainment; reader's contributions and
letters

Founded by the Worker's Publishing Cooperative in 1949 as a
fortnightly for children in the scouting movement, *Swiat Mlodych* is
now published three times a week. The magazine also publishes a
monthly edition for children of Polish origin living abroad.

Camacuc

Publisher: J.J.2-s.l.
Apartat de Correus, 11007
46080 València
Spain

For ages 6 to 14
10 issues per year
11,100 copies sold per issue
Format: 32 pages; black and color/full color sections;
21 x 32 cm; stapled
Editor-in-Chief: Joan Escrivà Torres
Art Directors: J. Escrivà, Jl. Matá
Editorial mission: to entertain and to provide children with the
opportunity to use the Catalan language and learn about the Catalan
culture
Editorial content: literature, fantasy, nature, science, education,
local news, crafts, comics, puzzles; children's contributions
and letters

Camacuc was founded in 1984 by a group of teachers who were
concerned about the language usage and culture of the Valencia
region. It is a Catalan-language magazine. Its mascot is a funny
little doll.

Caracola (Snail)

Publisher: SM&B, Hispano Francesa de Ediciones, S.A.
C/. Maqueda No. 30
28024 Madrid
Spain

For ages 4 to 7
12 issues per year
11,000 copies sold per issue
Format: 40 pages; full color; 21.5 x 24.5 cm; stapled
Editor-in-Chief: Ramón Menéndez
Art Director: Ulises Wensell
Editorial mission: to educate children by amusing them
Editorial content: fantasy, nature, science, education, sports, comics, puzzles; children's art and letters

Caracola was founded in 1988 and is the Spanish version of the French magazine *Pomme d'Api*. Some of the pages are created in Spain. Ouique, Carolina, and Oscar are the three main characters in the monthly cartoon strips.

Leo-Leo

Publisher: SM&B, Hispano Francesa de Ediciones, S.A.
Princesa, 25
28008 Madrid
Spain

12 issues per year
Format: 68 pages; full color; 15.5 x 19 cm; perfect-bound
Editorial content: stories, puzzles, comics

Cavall Fort

Publisher: Revista per a Nois i Noies Cavall Fort S.A.
Lesseps, 33. int.
08023 Barcelona
Spain

For ages 10 to 15; typical reader is a child of the Catalan minority
24 issues per year
22,500 copies sold per issue
Format: 32 pages; black and color/full color sections; 20.5 x 28.5
cm; stapled
Editor-in-Chief: Albert Jané
Editorial mission: to provide reading material for Catalan children
Editorial content: literature, fantasy, nature, science, history,
science fiction, astronomy, art, sports, crafts, comics; readers'
stories and letters

Cavall Fort is a Catalan-language magazine begun by Catalan
professors in Barcelona in 1961, when Catalan culture was being
oppressed by Franco's regime. Its mascot is a drummer.

Ipurbeltz

Publisher: Erein
Avenida de Tolosa 107
20009 - Donostia
Spain

For ages 8 to 11
12 issues per year
6,000 copies sold per issue
Format: 32 pages; full color; 20.5 x 27.5 cm; stapled
Editor-in-Chief: Julen Lizundia
Art Directors: Antton Olariaga, Alvaro Machinbarrena
Editorial mission: to provide Basque literature for children and adults
Editorial content: fantasy, crafts, comics

Ipurbeltz was founded in 1977 by Julen Lizundia, Angel Lerchundi, and Antton Olariaga.

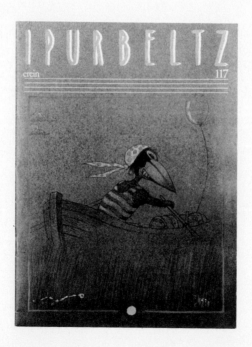

Pimpa

Publisher: Tebeos, S.A.
Ediciones B, Rocafort, 104
08015 Barcelona
Spain

For ages 4 to 10
12,500 copies sold per issue
Format: 32 pages; full color; 21 x 28 cm; stapled
Editor-in-Chief: Alberto Crespo
Art Director: Quipos, S.r.l.
Editorial content: general interest, comics; children's art and
letters

Pimpa was founded in 1988 by Quipos and is an adaptation of the
Italian magazine of the same name. The character Pimpa, a little
dog, appears in every issue.

Kamratposten (The Pal Post)

Publisher: Specialtidningsförlaget
Box 70452
10726 Stockholm
Sweden

For ages 8 to 14
18 issues per year
59,000 copies sold per issue
Format: 40 pages; full color; 20.5 x 26.5 cm; stapled
Editor-in-Chief: Christine von Hedenberg
Editorial mission: to provide children with sensible and jolly reading material
Editorial content: literature, nature, history, music, sports, crafts

Kamratposten was founded in 1892 by Stina Quint under the name *Elementary School*. The magazine has a teddy bear as its mascot.

Lyckoslanten (Lucky Penny)

Publisher: Sparfrämjandet AB
Sparbanken Kronan, Box 1217
S-351 12 Växjö
Sweden

For ages 5 to 14
4 issues per year
400,000 copies distributed per issue
Format: 24 pages; full color/black and white sections; 21 x 29.7 cm; stapled
Editor-in-Chief: Hans Barring
Art Director: Hans Barring
Editorial mission: to give children the impression that savings banks are friendly and effective, to teach children sound economic thinking, and to amuse and inform them with an interesting, varied content
Editorial content: general interest; children's contributions and letters

Lyckoslanten was founded in 1925 by a savings bank director in order to promote thrift among schoolchildren. It now promotes consumer knowledge and good economics.

Min Häst

Publisher: Semic Press/Bonnier Magazine Group
Box 74
172 22 Sundbyberg
Sweden

For ages 6 to 16; typical reader is an 11- to 14-year-old girl
26 issues per year
70,000 copies sold per issue
Format: 52 pages; full color; 17 x 26 cm; stapled
Editor-in-Chief: Catharina Hansson
Art Director: Eva Brangö
Editorial mission: to create an amusing and instructive magazine for young people who love horses
Editorial content: horses, riding; children's contributions and letters

Min Häst was founded in 1972 and is translated and printed in Holland, Denmark, and Finland. The cartoon figure Mulle appears regularly.

Zoo

Publisher: Semic/Bonnier Magazine Group
Box 74
172 22 Sundbyberg
Sweden

For ages 6 to 12; typical reader is a 9- to 11-year-old girl
12 issues per year
34,000 copies sold per issue
Format: 52 pages; full color; 16.7 x 26 cm; stapled
Editors: Noomi Hebert, Catharina Hansson
Art Director: Inger Ruta
Editorial mission: to provide entertaining and instructive reading material for children
Editorial content: animals, puzzles; children's contributions and letters

Zoo was founded in 1988 by Noomi Hebert and Catharina Hansson. It is translated and sold in Norway and Finland. Ziggy, a collie, is the magazine's mascot.

Jumi

Publisher: Katholische Kinder-Zeitschrift
5405 Immensee SZ
Switzerland

For ages 9 to 11
8 issues per year
75,000 copies sold per issue
Format: 24 pages; black and color; 17.5 x 21.5 cm; stapled
Editor-in-Chief: Sr. Maria Martha Schmid
Art Director: Mona Helle-Ineichen
Editorial mission: to provide interesting reading material about all
parts of the world and to break down prejudice that comes from a
lack of knowledge
Editorial content: literature, fantasy, nature, science, science
fiction, religion, anthropology, social science, crafts, comics,
puzzles; almost all original material; children's contributions and
letters

Jumi was founded in 1966 and is supported by fourteen missionary
institutes. A fantasy animal named Jumidil appears regularly in the
magazine's cartoon strip.

EUROPE

SWITZER-
LAND

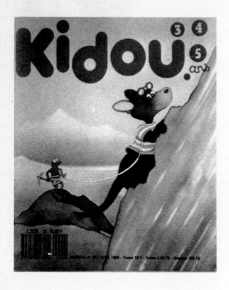

Kidou

Publisher: Editions Eiselé S.A.
17, Rue de Cossonay
1008 Prilly/Lausanne
Switzerland

For ages 3 to 5
12 issues per year
50,000 copies sold per issue
Format: 32 pages; full color; 17.5 x 21 cm; stapled
Editor-in-Chief: Andre Eiselé
Editorial mission: to educate children
Editorial content: fantasy, nature, sports

Kidou is a French-language publication founded in 1987. It is available in a German edition, *Kängi,* and has a kangaroo as its mascot.

Kodi

Publisher: Editions Eiselé S.A.
17, Rue de Cossonay
1008 Prilly/Lausanne
Switzerland

For ages 5 to 8
12 issues per year
50,000 copies sold per issue
Format: 36 pages; full color; 21 x 23.5 cm; stapled
Editor-in-Chief: André Eiselé
Editorial mission: to educate children
Editorial content: literature, fantasy, nature, science, sports, crafts

Kodi was founded in 1975 and has a bear as a mascot.

L'Aviöl

Publisher: Stamparia Engiadinaisa Samedan
Mario Pult, Conferenza Generala Ladina
Ftan 7551
Switzerland

For ages 7 to 15
6 issues per year
1500 copies sold per issue
Format: 30 to 40 pages; black and white;
15.75 x 21.75 cm; stapled
Editor-in-Chief: Mario Pult
Editorial mission: to provide children with reading material and
activities
Editorial content: literature, fantasy, nature, art, music, social
science, sports, crafts, comics, puzzles; children's contributions
and letters

L'Aviöl began in 1919 as a one-page publication. It is written in
Romansh.

Le Petit Ami des Animaux
(The Little Friend of Animals)

Publisher: Foundation Hermann Russ
2003 Neuchâtel
Switzerland

For ages 8 to 13
10 issues per year
18,000 copies sold per issue
Format: 16 pages; black and color; 15 x 21 cm; stapled
Editors: P. Bauer, C. Duscher, E. Duscher
Art Director: J. Decrauzat
Editorial mission: to teach children about pet care and animals in general, and to develop a respect for all animals
Editorial content: nature, pets; readers' contributions and letters

Le Petit Ami des Animaux was founded in 1918 by Hermann Russ. It has been published continuously since that time.

Spick

Publisher: Tages Anzeiger AG
Spick ABO-Dienst Postfach 8036
Zürich
Switzerland

For ages 9 to 14
12 issues per year
52,000 copies sold per issue
Format: 36 pages; full color; 21 x 29.7 cm;
perfect-bound
Editor-in-Chief: Otmar and Angelika Bucher-Waldis
Art Director: Otmar Bucher
Editorial mission: to offer interesting stories in a way that's
delectable and easily digested; to provide "food for the mind" with
the proverbial "spoonful of sugar" to make it fun and interesting
Editorial content: articles and stories on carefully selected themes
(such as fantasy, nature, science, and environmental issues) which
readers can organize into twelve different files; children's contributions and letters

Angelika and Otmar Bucher-Waldis founded *Spick* in 1982. The
magazine has many different genres to appeal to all kinds of
interests. Special codes mark the difficulty levels of stories and
articles. A fictional frog and lapwing greet readers every month.

Tut

Publisher: Schweizerischer Jungwachtbund und Blauring
Postfach
6000 Luzern 5
Switzerland

For ages 9 to 15
24 issues per year
15,000 copies sold per issue
Format: 28 pages; black and color/full color pages;
17 x 24 cm; stapled
Editor-in-Chief: Blanca Steinmann
Art Directors: Martin Vollmeier, Urs Holzgang
Editorial mission: to entertain, to encourage children to be
independent, and to give them Christian values
Editorial content: religion; children's contributions and letters

Tut was founded in 1936 by Schweizerischer Jungwachtbund. The
comic figure Eumel appears regularly.

Yakari

Publisher: Union Druck Verlag
Avenue de la Gare 39
1001 Lausanne
Switzerland

For ages 6 to 10
12 issues per year
28,000 copies sold per issue
Format: 32 pages; full color; 17 x 21 cm; stapled
Editor-in-Chief: André Jobin
Editorial mission: "For the child, the best is still not enough."
—Goethe
Editorial content: literature, fantasy, nature, science, crafts,
comics, puzzles

Yakari was founded in 1974 by André Jobin. Yakari, a Sioux Indian
boy, is the magazine's mascot.

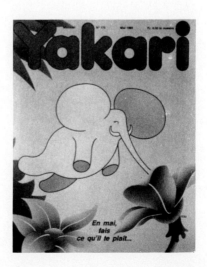

Ciciban

Publisher: Mladinska Knjiga
MK, Sok, Smartinska 152
61000 Ljubljana
Yugoslavia

For ages 3 to 7
11 issues per year
Format: 66 pages; full color; 15 x 21 cm; stapled
Editor-in-Chief: Bozo Kos
Art Director: Branka Schwarz
Editorial content: general interest; children's contributions
and letters

Ciciban was founded in 1945. It is published in Slovene and is a
nonprofit publication.

Kurircek
(The Little Messenger)

Publisher: Zalozba Borec
Miklosiceva 28
61000 Ljubljana
Yugoslavia

For ages 8 to 12
10 issues per year
30,000 copies sold per issue
Format: 32 to 64 pages; black and color/full color section; 20.5 x 26 cm; stapled
Editor-in-Chief: Boris A. Novak
Art Director: Boris A. Novak
Editorial mission: to help children see art as the childhood of the world and to see their own childhood as the art of life
Editorial content: literature; all original stories; children's contributions and letters

Zalozba Borec founded *Kurircek* in 1960 to celebrate national history, especially the liberation movement of Slovene and Yugoslav partisans against the Nazi occupation during World War II. Today it is purely a literary magazine.

Pionieri

Publisher: Vydavatelská Organizácia Tvorba
Obzor - Tvorba, Bulevar 23. Oktobra 31/V
Novi Sad 21000
Yugoslavia

For ages 8 to 13; typical reader is a village child
10 issues per year
7,500 copies sold per issue
Format: 24 pages; black and color/full color section; 19.5 x 26 cm;
stapled
Editor-in-Chief: Miroslav Demák
Art Director: Michal Királ
Editorial mission: to foster the language of the Slovak minority in
Yugoslavia
Editorial content: literature, fantasy, education, art, music, sports,
puzzles; children's art

Pionieri, a government-owned publication, was founded in 1939 by
Matica Slovenská. Every issue contains a 16-page insert called
Mravec for children ages 4 to 8.

Pionir

Publisher: Mladinska Knjiga
MK, Sok, Smartinska 152
61107 Ljubljana
Yugoslavia

For age 14 and older
10 issues per year
Format: 40 pages; black and color; 21 x 29.5 cm;
stapled
Editor-in-Chief: Sreco Zajc
Art Directors: Branka Schwarz, Ranko Novak
Editorial content: general interest

Pionir was first published in 1945. It is a nonprofit
Slovene-language publication.

PIL - Pionirski List

Publisher: Mladinska Knjiga
MK, Sok, Smartinska 152
61000 Ljubljana
Yugoslavia

For ages 7 to 15
Format: 34 pages; black and color; 22 x 29 cm; stapled
Editor-in-Chief: Valter Samide
Art Director: Màrjan Rombo
Editorial mission: to educate and entertain
Editorial content: general interest; children's letters

PIL is a Slovene-language publication.

Titov Pionir

Publisher: Savjet Za Staranje O Djeci Crne Gore
ul. V. Djurovica bb - post. fah. 163
81.000 Titograd
Yugoslavia

For ages 7 to 14
10 issues per year
130,000 copies sold per issue
Format: 32 pages; black and color/full color section; 20.4 x 28.5 cm; stapled
Editor-in-Chief: Nada Kosovic
Art Director: Sveto Martinovic
Editorial mission: to educate and amuse
Editorial content: general interest, education; children's contributions and letters

The Youth Organization of Montenegro founded
Titov Pionir in 1950.

USSR

Barvinok

Publisher: Publishing House Molod (Youth)
Str. Parchomenko, 38-44
Kiev-119
USSR 252119

For ages 6 to 10
12 issues per year
1,110,000 copies sold per issue
Format: 24 pages; full color; 21.5 x 28.5 cm; stapled
Editor-in-Chief: Vasil Moruga
Art Director: Konstantin Lavro
Editorial mission: to serve the ongoing crucial restructuring process (*perestroika*); to teach children national history and traditions; and to return to the original folk spirit of the Ukranian people
Editorial content: general interest and literature; children's contributions and letters

The Young Communist League of the Ukraine founded *Barvinok* in 1928 under the name *Jovtenya*. Before 1950, the magazine was written in Ukrainian. It is now also available in Russian. Its name is that of a little flower.

Druzhba (Friendship)

Publisher: Molodaya Gvardia (Young Communist League)
Novodmitrovskaya 5a
125015 Moscow
USSR

For ages 7 to 18
6 issues per year
86,000 copies sold per issue
Format: 160 pages; black and color; 14 x 21 cm; stapled
Editor-in-Chief: Firsov Vladimir Ivanovich
Art Director: Dunko V.V.
Editorial Mission: to strengthen friendship between the Soviet and Bulgarian peoples and among all peoples of the world
Editorial content: general interest; readers' contributions and letters

Druzhba was first published in 1977.

Kipina (Spark)

Publisher: Karelia
Petrozavodsk, Karelia
USSR

For elementary school children
Format: 24 pages; full color; 21.2 x 27.3 cm; stapled
Editor-in-Chief: Viktor Husu
Art Director: Nikolai Truhin
Editorial content: stories, songs, puzzles; children's contributions

Kolobok

Publisher: Pravda Gosteleradio SSSR
Pyatnitskaya Ulitsa 25
113326 Moscow
USSR

For ages 3 to 9; typical reader is 5 to 12
12 issues per year
540,000 copies sold per issue
Format: 16 pages; full color; 20 x 28.5 cm; stapled
Editor-in-Chief: Boris Hessin
Art Director: Oleg Koznov
Editorial mission: to encourage children to be kind, fair, compassionate, and caring for all living things; to stimulate the desire to learn about and appreciate beauty and art
Editorial content: general interest, songs, two records included in every issue; children's contributions and letters

Kolobok, a government-owned publication, was founded in 1969 by the State Committee for Television and Radio Broadcasting. The magazine is very popular in the USSR and abroad. Kolobok, the magazine's hero, is a cheerful, curious, round piece of bread that rolls wherever it wants.

Komsomolskaya Zhizn (Komsomol Life)

Publisher: Central Committee of the Komsomol
Novodmitrovskaya 5a
125015 Moscow
USSR

For ages 14 to 25; typical reader is a male student or worker who is concerned with peers' interests and politics
24 issues per year
920,000 copies sold per issue
Format: 32 pages; black and color; 14 x 21 cm; stapled
Editor-in-Chief: Aleksej Shevelev
Art Directors: V. Pzesnyakov, T. Mazakulina
Editorial mission: to provide information
Editorial content: general interest including social activities; readers' contributions and letters

Komsomolskaya Zhizn was first published by the Soviet Komsomol in 1920. It has 50,000 subscribers in 31 countries outside the USSR.

Kostyor (Bonfire)

Publisher: Central Committee of the Young Communist League, the Central Council of the Lenin Pioneer Organization, and the Writers' Union of the USSR
Mytninskaya ul. 1/20
193024 Leningrad
USSR

For ages 9 to 13
12 issues per year
1,330,000 copies sold per issue
Format: 49 pages; full color/black and color; 21.2 x 28.4 cm; stapled
Editor-in-Chief: O.A. Tsakunov
Art Director: A.N. Azemsha
Editorial mission: to publish contemporary fictional works by Soviet authors, translations of foreign literature, and classical literature
Editorial content: literature, science, nature, sports, musical and literary discussions, history of the USSR, games, comics, riddles; children's contributions and letters

Kostyor began publication in 1936.

Murzilka

Publisher: Molodaya Gvardia (Young Communist League)
Novodmitrovskaya 5a
125015 Moscow
USSR

For ages 6 to 11
12 issues per year
5,200,000 copies sold per issue
Format: 32 pages; full color; 20 x 26 cm; stapled
Editor-in-Chief: Tatiana Androsenko
Art Director: Alexander Shliandin
Editorial Mission: to provide science material and fiction for children
Editorial content: literature, nature, science, foreign countries, Soviet festivals, history, sports, art, comics, puzzles, songs; children's contributions and letters

Murzilka was first published by the Young Communist League in 1924.

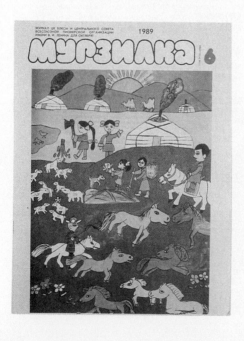

Noorus (Youth)

Publisher: Central Committee of the Estonian Young Communist League
Tallinn, Estonia
USSR

For ages 14 to 18
108,000 copies sold per issue
Format: 42 pages; black and color; 20 x 28 cm; stapled
Editor-in-Chief: Lida Jarve

Noorus began publication in 1946. It is published in the Estonian language.

Pioneer

Publisher: Central Committee of the Armenian Young Communist League
Erivan, Armenia
USSR

For ages 12 to 18
63,652 copies sold per issue
Format: 34 pages; full color/black and color; 16.5 x 24 cm; stapled

Pioneer is written in Armenian.

Pioner (Pioneer)

Publisher: Central Committee of the Young Communist League and the Lenin Pioneer Organization
Bumazhny Proyezd 14
101459 Moscow
USSR

For ages 9 to 13
12 issues per year
1,770,000 copies sold per issue
Format: 65 pages; full color; 20 x 28.2 cm; stapled
Editor-in-Chief: A.S. Moroz
Art Director: A.M. Grishin
Editorial content: literature, articles on Pioneer and school life, history, sports, science, foreign countries; children's contributions and letters

Pioner started publication in 1924. It sponsors many competitions and quizzes for its readers.

Vesyoliye Kartinki (Merry Pictures)

Publisher: Central Committee of the Young Communist League
Novodmitrovskaya 5a
125015 Moscow
USSR

For ages 3 to 7
12 issues per year
9,150,000 copies sold per issue
Format: 16 pages; full color; 20 x 26 cm; stapled
Editor-in-Chief: Ruben A. Varshamov
Art Director: Sergey Tunin
Editorial content: stories and poems by Soviet and foreign contemporary writers, Russian folk tales, fairy tales, riddles, games, puzzles, comics; all original illustrations

Vesyoliye Kartinki was founded in 1956 by Ivan Semenov.

Yuni Khudozhnik
(Young Artist)

Publisher: Molodaya Gvardia (Young Communist League)
Novodmitrovskaya 5a
125015 Moscow
USSR

For ages 10 and up
12 issues per year
185,000 copies sold per issue
Format: 48 pages; black and color; 19.5 x 24.5 cm; stapled
Editor-in-Chief: L.A. Shitov
Art Director: A.K. Zaytsev
Editorial content: art; readers' art, photographs, and letters

Yuni Khudozhnik was first published in 1936.

Yuni Naturalist
(Young Naturalist)

Publisher: Molodaya Gvardia (Young Communist League)
Novodmitrovskaya 5a
125015 Moscow
USSR

For ages 10 to 16
12 issues per year
3,000,000 copies sold per issue
Format: 48 pages; full color; 16.5 x 23 cm; stapled
Editor-in-Chief: N.N. Starchenko
Art Director: A.A. Tyurin
Editorial mission: to provide information about ecology
and the history of life on Earth
Editorial content: nature, science; children's
contributions and letters

Yuni Naturalist is a popular science magazine that began
publication in 1928. It is the first children's magazine in the
USSR devoted entirely to ecological education. The magazine has initiated many nature conservation campaigns by
schoolchildren and nurtured a national movement of young
naturalists.

Yuni Tekhnik

Publisher: Molodaya Gvardia (Young Communist
League)
Novodmitrovskaya 5a
125015 Moscow
USSR

For ages 11 to 17
12 issues per year
1,850,000 copies sold per issue
Format: 80 pages; black and color; 12.3 x 20 cm;
perfect-bound
Editor-in-Chief: Sukhomlinov V.V.
Art Director: Ivanoba O.M.
Editorial content: fantasy, science, history, science
fiction, astronomy, sports, crafts, puzzles; readers' contributions and letters

Yuni Tekhnik was founded by Bolkhobitinov V.N. in 1956.

Vokrug Sveta
(Around the World)

Publisher: Molodaya Gvardia (Young Communist
League)
Novodmitrovskaya 5a
125015 Moscow
USSR

For ages 11 and up
12 issues per year
3,000,000 copies sold per issue
Format: 64 pages; full color/black and white;
20 x 26 cm; perfect-bound
Editor-in-Chief: Alexandr Poleshchuk
Art Director: Vladimir Nevolin
Editorial mission: to publish stories and articles about
travels and adventures
Editorial content: literature, nature, science, history,
science fiction, astronomy; all original articles and stories

Vokrug Sveta was founded in 1861 by Mavriky Volf, a
book publisher. It ceased publication from 1917 to 1927
and again during the war years of 1941-45. It has been
published continuously since 1946.

Täheka (Star)

Publisher: Publishing House of the Estonian Communist Party
Kreutzwaldi 12 Ajakirjanduslevi
200109 Tallinn, Estonia
USSR

For ages 6 to 10
12 issues per year
78,000 copies sold per issue
Format: 16 pages; full color; 21.5 x 28 cm; stapled
Editor-in-Chief: Elju Mardi
Art Director: Jaan Tammsaar
Editorial mission: to be a friend and an adviser to children
Editorial content: literature, nature, history, puzzles; children's
contributions and letters

Täheke was founded in 1960 by the Estonian Young Communist
League and is published in Estonian.

Trukitahed (Print)

Publisher: Eesti Raamat
Tallinn, Estonia
USSR

For ages 12 to 14
Format: 96 pages; black and white; 19.5 x 28 cm; perfect-bound
Editor-in-Chief: V. Parvo
Art Director: Evi Sepp
Editorial content: literature and illustrations created by students

Trukitahed is written in the Estonian language.

Vyasyolka

Publisher: Central Committee of the Communist Party of Belorussia
10 Kollektornaya St.
Minsk 220084
USSR

For ages 5 to 10
12 issues per year
100,100 copies sold per issue
Format: 16 pages; full color; 20 x 28.5 cm; stapled
Editor-in-Chief: Vladimir Stepanovich Lipsky
Art Director: Evgeny Alekseyevich Larchenko
Editorial mission: the upbringing and education of children
Editorial content: literature, nature, history, art, music, puzzles; children's letters

Vyasyolka was founded by Vasil' Vitka in 1957. It prints not only the best works of Belorussian writers, but also those of many brothering republics and socialist countries, in Russian. The magazine is read not only by children, but also by teachers and librarians. Its mascot is Vasya Vesyolkin, the magazine's hero.

AFRICA

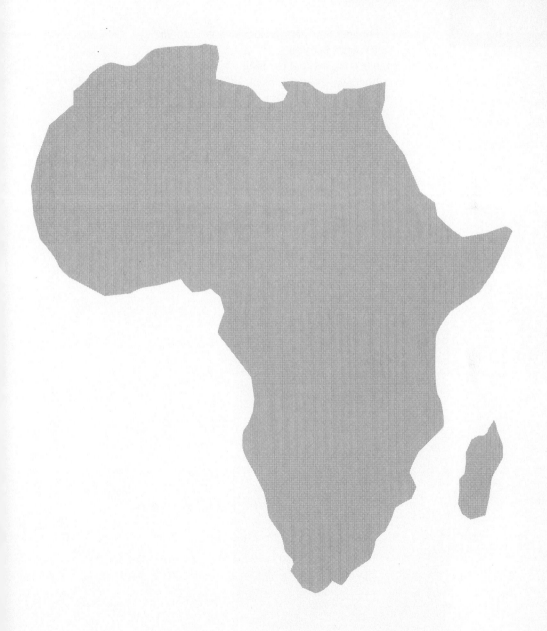

Ngouvou (Hippopotamus)

Publisher: Bob Lhomme
B.P. 2351
Brazzaville
Congo

For ages 8 to 16; typical reader is 12 to 16
10 issues per year
6,000 copies sold per issue
Format: 24 pages; black and white; 21x 29.5 cm; stapled
Editor-in-Chief: Bob Lhomme
Art Director: Tchïbemba
Editorial mission: to provide children with an educational and entertaining magazine
Editorial content: general interest; children's contributions and letters

Founded in 1988 by Bob Lhomme and N. Richard, *Ngouvou* is the only children's magazine in the Congo. A hippopotamus is the magazine's mascot.

Sadouk El Donia

Publisher: Egyptian Society for the Dissemination of Universal
Culture & Knowledge
1081, Cornish el Nil
Garden City, Cairo
Egypt

For ages 10 to 14
12 issues per year
5,000 copies sold per issue
Format: 20 pages; full color/black and color pages; 20 x 27 cm;
stapled
Editor-in-Chief: Inas Effat
Editorial mission: to offer the Arab child a magazine promoting
national morals and ideals and to provide general knowledge
Editorial content: comics, science, science fiction; children's
contributions and letters

Sandouk El Donia was founded by the Egyptian Society for the
Dissemination of Universal Culture & Knowledge in 1978. It is
published in collaboration with *Youth, Science & Future*, published
by Al Ahram.

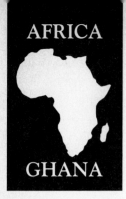

Playpen

Publisher: Pluto Publications
P.O. Box 14935
Accra
Ghana

For ages 7 to 14; typical reader is a private school student
12 issues per year
10,200 copies sold per issue
Format: 20 pages; black and white; 21 x 30.75 cm; stapled
Editor-in-Chief: Senna Tagboto
Art Director: Eric Djomoah
Editorial mission: to cultivate the habit of reading and learning in children and to broaden their knowledge of the world around them
Editorial content: education; children's contributions

Playpen was founded by Senna Tagboto in 1989. Its challenge is to reach public school children, whose parents often do not realize the importance of supplementary educational material and cannot afford it. Bibi is a character who appears in each issue's comic section.

The Child

Publisher: Fegann Communications Ltd.
P.O. Box 12556
Accra-North
Ghana

For ages 5 to 16
6 issues per year
Format: 8 pages; black and white; 21 x 29 cm; stapled
Editor-in-Chief: Felix E. Gaba
Art Director: Kwame Roi Kuwornu
Editorial mission: to encourage children to enjoy reading and
writing
Editorial content: literature, history, comics, all original stories
and illustrations; children's contributions and letters

The Child was started by Felix E. Gaba in 1986. Responses from
pupils and teachers are encouraging, but production targets have not
been met due to lack of printing equipment and transportation. *The
Child* is embarking on a nationwide promotion.

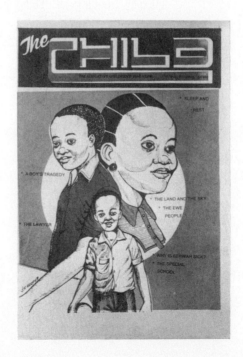

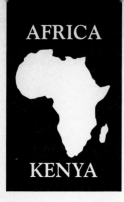

AFRICA

KENYA

Rainbow

Publisher: Stellagraphics Limited
P.O. Box 42271
Nairobi
Kenya

For ages 10 to 16; typical reader is a 13-year-old serious student
from a small town
12 issues per year
11,500 copies sold per issue
Format: 32 pages; black and white/full color sections; 19 x 28 cm;
stapled
Editor-in-Chief: Fleur Ng'weno
Art Director: Arabron Osanya-Nyyneque
Editorial mission: to help children understand the world around
them, and to provide stimulating reading material to children who
speak English as a second language
Editorial content: general interest, nature, puzzles, activities,
news; readers' contributions and letters

Rainbow was started in 1976 by Hilary and Fleur Ng'weno to
provide non-imperialistic English-language reading material for
children. Originally, the magazine purchased cartoon strips and
puzzles from abroad. Today it contains all local material.

Asha

Publisher: Kema Chikwe
Prime Time Ltd., No. 20 Valley Crescent
Plot 627, Independence Layout
Enugu, Anambra State
Nigeria

For ages 12 to 17
4 issues per year
Format: 50 pages; black and white/full color section; 21 x 29.5 cm;
stapled
Editorial Director: Kema Chikwe
Art Director: Linus Okasi
Editorial mission: to provide a quality magazine that is of interest
to children and to develop the reading culture, particularly in Nigeria
Editorial content: general interest; children's contributions and
letters

Asha was first published by Kema Chikwe in 1985 in London. It is
now published in Nigeria, in English, the official language of that
country.

The Junior Group Magazine

Publisher: The Group
U.I. P.O. Box 9559
Ibadan
Nigeria

For ages 6 to 16
3 issues per year
Format: 50 pages; black and white; 20 x 25 cm; stapled
Editor-in-Chief: Dapo Awotedu
Art Director: Funso Onafowokan
Editorial mission: to encourage readers to express themselves
Editorial content: general interest; children's contributions

The Junior Group Magazine was first published in 1990 by The Group, an organization of professionals, business people and civil servants in and around the University of Ibadan, as a forum for their children to express their literary and artistic talents. It is nonprofit.

VOL 1 NO 1 APRIL 1990

Junior Bob Magazine

Publisher: First National Bank
P.O. Box 32710
Braamfontein 2017
South Africa

For ages 8 to 12
6 issues per year
200,000 copies sold per issue
Format: 20 to 24 pages; full color; 21 x 28 cm; stapled
Editor-in-Chief: Simone Kaplan
Art Director: Nicole Sinoff
Editorial mission: to stimulate, entertain, and inform children about a great variety of subjects in order to initiate self-discovery
Editorial content: education, stories; children's contributions and letters

Junior Bob was started by the First National Bank in 1985. It is distributed to every bank account holder. Its mascots are the Bobbits.

T-Magazine

Publisher: First National Bank
P.O. Box 32710
Braamfontein, 2017
South Africa

For ages 12 to 18; typical reader is a 16-year-old
English-speaking male
6 issues per year
230,000 copies sold per issue
Format: 36 to 52 pages; full color; 21 x 28 cm; stapled
Editor-in-Chief: Simone Kaplan
Art Director: Nicole Sinoff
Editorial mission: to entertain and promote New Age
ideas
Editorial content: general interest; children's contributions

T-Magazine was founded by the First National Bank in
1985.

Skipper

Publisher: Department of Environment Affairs
Private Bag X447
Pretoria, 0001
South Africa

For ages 6 to 17
10 to12 issues per year
66,000 copies sold per issue
Format: 12 to 16 pages; full color; 20.5 x 29.75 cm;
stapled
Editor-in-Chief: Nicolene Botha
Editorial mission: to teach children about the environment and to create love and respect for it
Editorial content: environment; children's questions

Skipper was started by the Department of Environment
Affairs in 1981. It is government owned. Each issue
focuses on a geographical or environmental theme. A
boy named Skipper and his friends are the mascots.

Toktokkie

Publisher: Wildlife Society of Southern Africa
P.O. Box 44189
Linden 2104
South Africa

For ages 7 to 13
6 issues per year
12,500 copies sold per issue
Format: 24 pages; black and color/full color sections; 21 x 29.5 cm; stapled
Editor-in-Chief: Deirdre Richards
Editorial mission: to provide enjoyable natural history and conservation education
Editorial content: nature, original photographs and illustrations; children's contributions and letters

Toktokkie was started in 1976 as a children's section in the adult periodical *African Wildlife*. Due to an increasing interest in environmental education and the formation of wildlife clubs, *Toktokkie* became a separate magazine in 1980.

Youngtime

Publisher: Shot Publishers
P.O. Box 262
Johannesburg 2000
South Africa

For ages 6 to 14; typical reader is 11
12 issues per year
9,500 copies sold per issue
Format: 48 pages; full color; 19.5 x 27 cm; stapled
Editor: Sonja Weiss
Art Director: Rob Hooper
Editorial mission: to encourage children to read, learn, and think, and to entertain
Editorial content: education, geography, health, psychology, pen pals, pop stars; children's contributions and letters

Youngtime was started by Kevin Picker and Hazel Cohn in 1985. The editors encourage children to submit their own work in the hope that eventually at least 25% of the magazine will be written by children.

Malihai

Publisher: Malihai Clubs of Tanzania
P.O. Box 1541
Arusha
Tanzania

For ages 15 and older
2 issues per year
Format: 28 pages; black and white; 20.6 x 29.6 cm; stapled
Editor-in-Chief: Peter A. Ottaru
Editorial mission: to provide environmental education
Editorial content: nature, science, education, puzzles; readers' contributions and letters

Dr. Janette Hanby Bygott founded *Malihai Magazine* in 1982.

AFRICA

ZAIRE

Ndotsi (News)

Publisher: Lycée Nsang'ea Ndotsi
B.P. 453
Mbandaka
Zaire

For ages 14 to 20
1 issue per year
Format: 12 pages; black and white; 21 x 29.7 cm; stapled
Editor-in-Chief: Eva Meinerts
Editorial mission: to introduce the idea of writing and reading one's own articles
Editorial content: general interest including social science, sports, comics; entirely written and illustrated by students

Ndotsi is a school publication that first came out in the 1970s. It is published whenever the pupils and teachers are eager to create another issue.

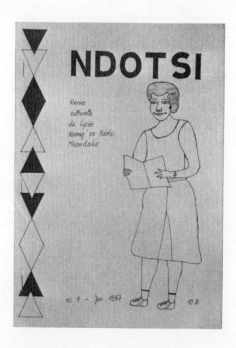

MIDDLE EAST

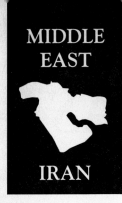

MIDDLE
EAST

IRAN

Ayesh

Publisher: Kanun Parvaresh Fekri Kudakan va Nojavanan
P.O. Box 14335-5885
Tehran
Iran

For ages 12 to 17
12 issues per year
42,000 copies sold per issue
Format: 48 pages; full color; 22 x 29 cm; stapled
Editor-in-Chief: Vahid Toofani
Art Director: Mohammad Reza Dadgar
Editorial mission: to help young people develop their creativity
Editorial content: literature; reader's contributions and letters

Ayesh was founded in 1984 by the Center for Literary Creativities. It is government owned and almost entirely comprised of readers' stories, articles, poems, and art.

Kavosh

Publisher: Kanun Parvaresh Fekri Kudakan va Nojavanan
P.O. Box 14335-5885
Tehran
Iran

For ages 12 to 17
4 issues per year
30,200 copies sold per issue
Format: 48 pages; full color; 22 x 29 cm; stapled
Editor-in-Chief: Vahid Toofani
Art Director: Mohammad Reza Dadgar
Editorial mission: to acquaint young people with the applied sciences
Editorial content: science, astronomy

Kavosh is a government-owned publication which was founded by
Reza Rohani in 1984.

Kushesh

Publisher: Kanun Parvaresh Fekri Kudakan va Nojavanan
P.O. Box 14335-588
Tehran
Iran

For ages 9 to 15
8 issues per year
30,500 copies sold per issue
Format: 30 pages; full color; 24 x 32 cm; stapled
Editor-in-Chief: Vahid Toofani
Art Director: Mohammad Reza Dadgar
Editorial mission: to give children creative work to do in their spare time and to make them more aware of their talents
Editorial content: art, crafts, puzzles; children's contributions and letters

Kushesh was founded in 1988 by the Hobbies & Toys Center and is government owned.

Fonoun (Technology)

Publisher: Ing Saïd Berenjchi
Khajeh Nassir Str. 257, P.O. Box 11365-4466
Tehran
Iran

For ages 9 to 16
12 issues per year
7,100 copies sold per issue
Format: 52 pages; black and color; 21 x 28 cm; stapled
Editors: Ing S. Berenjchi, Mr. Khakbazan
Art Director: Abdollahzadeh
Editorial mission: to provide young people with scientific articles
Editorial content: nature, science, science fiction, education, astronomy, art, social science, crafts, comics, crosswords, competitions for construction of technological devices; children's contributions and letters

Fonoun was founded in 1989 by Ing S. Berenjchi.

Keyhan Bacheha (Children's Keyhan)

Publisher: Keyhan Institut
Ferdowsi Str., Atabak Lane
Tehran
Iran

For ages 6 to 16
51 issues per year
70,000 copies sold per issue
Format: 46 pages; full color; 17 x 24 cm; stapled
Editor-in-Chief: Amir Hossein Fardi
Art Directors: Rassoul Fallahpour, Fariba Aflatoun
Editorial mission: to provide a magazine directed by the needs, aspirations, aptitudes, and capabilities of children
Editorial content: literature, astronomy, art, religion, social science, sports, crafts, comics, puzzles; children's contributions and letters

Keyhan Bacheha was founded in 1956 by Abbas Yamini Sharif. Before the Islamic Revolution, the magazine relied heavily on translated stories and illustrations by foreign artists. Today it is prepared by young Iranian authors and artists.

Keyhan Elmi Baraye Nowjavanan
(Scientific Keyhan for Young People)

Publisher: Keyhan Institut
Ferdowsi Str., Shahcheraghi Lane
Tehran
Iran

For ages 13 to 17
12 issues per year
20,000 copies sold per issue
Format: 52 pages; black and color; 21 x 28 cm; stapled
Editors: Amir Hossein Fardi, F. Hosseinzadeh
Editorial mission: to acquaint young people with the scientific
method and to teach them about the environment
Editorial content: nature, science, history, astronomy, anthropology, social science, crafts; children's contributions and letters

Keyhan Elmi Baraye Nowjavanan was founded in 1989 by Amir
Fardi.

Roshd Now Amouz (Beginner's Growth)

Publisher: Ministry of Education
P.O. Box 15875
3331 Tehran
Iran

For ages 6 to 8
9 issues per year
600,000 copies sold per issue
Format: 16 pages; full color; 21 x 28 cm; stapled
Editor-in-Chief: Hamid Gerogan
Art Director: Mohammad Ali Keshavarz
Editorial mission: to establish and develop reading habits and to implement the educational objectives formulated by the Ministry of Education
Editorial content: literature, nature, science, history, education, art, religion, social science, sports, crafts, comics, puzzles; children's contributions and letters

Roshd Now Amouz, a government-owned publication, was founded by the Ministry of Education in 1967 under the name *Peik Now Amouz.* After the Islamic Revolution, the magazine changed its name and began to emphasize Islamic thought and education.

Roshd Danesh Amouz (Pupil's Growth)

Publisher: Ministry of Education
P.O. Box 15875
3331 Tehran
Iran

For ages 9 to 12
9 issues per year
600,000 copies sold per issue
Format: 32 pages; full color; 21 x 28 cm; stapled
Editor-in-Chief: Mostafa Rahmandoust
Art Director: Mohammad Ali Keshavarz
Editorial mission: to develop good reading skills and habits and to promote the educational objectives formulated by the Ministry of Education
Editorial content: science, literature, nature, history, art, religion, social science, sports, crafts, puzzles; children's contributions and letters

Roshd Danesh Amouz, a government-owned publication, was founded by the Ministry of Education in 1964 under the name *Peik.* It changed its name after the Islamic Revolution and began to emphasize politics and religion.

Roshd Nowjavan (Adolescent's Growth)

Publisher: Ministry of Education
P.O. Box 15875
3331 Tehran
Iran

For ages 12 to 16
9 issues per year
400,000 copies sold per issue
Format: 48 pages; full color; 21 x 28 cm; stapled
Editor-in-Chief: Ahmad Arablou
Art Director: Mohammad Ali Keshavarz
Editorial mission: to give pupils a broader outlook on life, art vocations, science, and creative activities
Editorial content: general interest; children's contributions and letters

Roshd Nowjavan, a government-owned publication, was founded by the Ministry of Education in 1972 under the name *Peik Nowjavanan.* It changed its name after the Islamic Revolution and began to emphasize politics, religion, and morality.

Youth's Roshd
(Youth's Growth)

Publisher: Ministry of Education
P.O. Box 15875/3331
Tehran
Iran

For ages 15 to 20
9 issues per year
270,000 copies sold per issue
Format: 84 pages; black and color; 20 x 28 cm; stapled
Editor-in-Chief: Seyed Mehdi Shojaee
Art Director: Kamran Mehrzadeh
Editorial content: science, literature, history, education, art, religion, anthropology, sports, crafts, puzzles; readers' letters

Youth's Roshd, a government-owned publication, was founded in 1984 under the name *Youth's Payk* by the Ministry of Education. It changed its name after the Islamic Revolution.

Soroush Nowjavan
(Soroush for Young Adults)

Publisher: Soroush
Ostad Motahari Str., Jâm Jam Building
Tehran
Iran

For ages 12 to 16
12 issues per year
30,000 copies sold per issue
Format: 52 pages; black and white; 21.5 x 28 cm; stapled
Editors: Gh. Aminpour, F. Amouzadeh Khalili, B. Maleki
Editorial mission: to provide an artistic literary magazine for young people
Editorial content: literature, science, art, anthropology; children's contributions and letters

Soroush Nowjavan was founded in 1988 by an editorial board. It is an independent magazine financed by a semi-governmental institution.

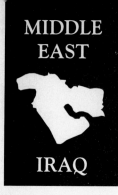

MIDDLE EAST

IRAQ

Majalati

Publisher: House for Children's Culture
Salhiyya - P.O. Box 8041
Baghdad
Iraq

For ages 5 to 14
52 issues per year
35,700 copies sold per issue
Format: 40 pages; full color/black and white;
23 x 29 cm; stapled
Editor-in-Chief: Farouq Saloom
Art Director: Riyadh Al Salim
Editorial content: general interest; children's contributions and
letters

Majalati is a government-owned publication that was founded by
the Ministry of Information and Culture in 1969.

Kulanu

Publisher: Kulanu Ltd.
2 Homa Umigdal St.
Tel Aviv 61999
Israel

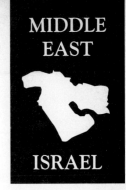

For ages 8 to 12
52 issues per year
45,000 copies sold per issue
Format: 48 pages; full color; 22 x 30.2 cm; stapled
Editor-in-Chief: David Faians
Art Directors: Suzy Baruch, Lena Rabinovitch
Editorial mission: to be a child's friend
Editorial content: general interest; children's contributions and letters

Kulanu was founded by Davar Haaretz and Al Hamishmar in 1985.

Kulanu Alef Bet

Publisher: Kulanu
2 Homa Umigdal St.
Telaviv 61999
Israel

For ages 6 to 8
26 issues per year
Format: 24 pages; full color; 22 x 30.4 cm; stapled
Editor-in-Chief: David Faians
Art Director: Roni Kurtz
Editorial content: general interest

Kulanu Alef Bet was begun by Kulanu in 1989.

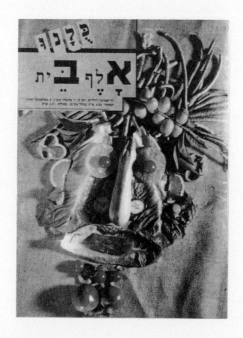

Pilon

Publisher: Pilon Publishers
Yehuda Halevi 4
Tel Aviv 65135
Israel

For ages 6 to 10
Format: 32 pages; black and color/full color section;
23 x 27.5 cm; stapled
Editor-in-Chief: Nurit Yuval
Art Director: Cesar Asher
Editorial mission: to provide children with articles about culture,
humor, and general knowledge
Editorial content: stories, puzzles, crosswords, rhymes, comics

Pilon was founded by the Massada Publishing House in 1979.

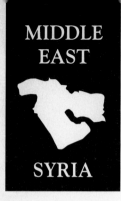

Ousama (Boys)

Publisher: Ministry of Culture
Damascus
Syria

For ages 9 to 12
12 issues per year
49,000 copies sold per issue
Format: 24 pages; full color/black and color;
20 x 27 cm; stapled
Editor-in-Chief: Dalal Hatem
Art Director: Liass Hamoue
Editorial content: literature, fantasy, nature, science, history,
science fiction, education, astronomy, art, sports, crafts, comics,
puzzles; children's contributions and letters

The Ministry of Culture founded *Ousama* in 1969. The boy
character Ex-Syah appears regularly in the magazine.

Bando

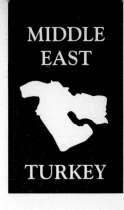

Publisher: Gelisim Yayinlari A.S.
Levent
Istanbul
Turkey

For ages 7 to 14
12 issues per year
50,000 copies sold per issue
Format: 32 pages; full color; 19.5 x 27; stapled
Editor-in-Chief: Yalvaç Ural
Art Director: Sahin Erkoçak
Editorial mission: to give children a cultural education by
providing them with articles of national and traditional importance
Editorial content: nature, animals, literature, crafts, art, social
science, comics, anthropology, games; children's contributions and
letters

Bando was founded in 1988 by Ercan Arikli. A little girl, her dog,
and their poet friend appear in every issue.

Dogan Kardes

Publisher: Yapi Kredi Yayinlari Ltd.
Mesrutiyet Caddesi 153 Tepebasi
80050 Istanbul
Turkey

For ages 9 to 14
12 issues per year
39,000 copies sold per issue
Format: 68 pages; full color; 20 x 27 cm; stapled
Editor-in-Chief: M. Turhan Ilgaz
Art Director: Erdogan Ugurlu
Editorial mission: to contribute to the formation of open-minded
and peace-loving children and to encourage them to have an
international scope
Editorial content: general interest; original stories and art; children's contributions and letters

Kazim Taskent founded *Dogan Kardes* in 1945 in memory of his
son Dogan Taskent. The magazine ceased publication in 1975 due
to organizational problems and started again in 1988 in a new
format.

Kirmizifare (The Red Mouse)

Publisher: Redhouse Press
Pk. 142 Sirkeci
34432 Istanbul
Turkey

For ages 8 to 12
Format: 32 pages; black and color; 18 x 22.75 cm; stapled
Editor-in-Chief: Fatih Erdogan
Graphic Artist: Feridun Oral
Editorial mission: to provide quality literature and illustrations for children
Editorial content: literature, puzzles

Kirmizifare was first published in March 1990, as a quarterly. The publisher has plans for it to become a bimonthly in 1991 and a monthly in 1992.

Majed

Publisher: Al Ittihad Printing and Publishing Corp.
P.O. Box 3558
Abu Dhabi
United Arab Emirates

For ages 6 to 16
52 issues per year
171,000 copies sold per issue
Format: 56 pages; full color/black and color section;
20 x 27.5 cm; stapled
Editor-in-Chief: Abdullah Al Nowais
Art Director: Ahmed Hijazi
Editorial mission: to raise a generation of mature readers who
believe in God and a unified Arab world
Editorial content: general interest; children's contributions and
letters

Majed was founded in 1979 by Ahmed Omar. The magazine is
available in most Arab countries and has very loyal readers. The
editorial staff often takes readers' opinions into consideration.

FAR EAST ASIA

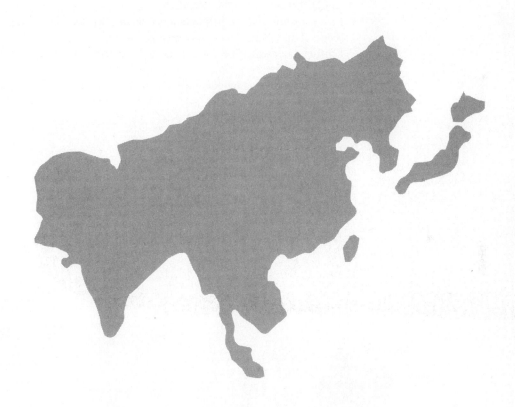

Baby Pictorial

Publisher: Juvenile and Children Publishing House
P.O. Box 2820 (Book Code No. M758)
Beijing
People's Republic of China

For ages 2 to 4
12 issues per year
300,000 copies sold per issue
Format: 24 pages; full color; 19 x 17 cm; stapled
Editor-in-Chief: Zhen Ma
Art Directors: Zhou He, Zhang Jun
Editorial mission: to help toddlers cultivate wisdom, broaden their scope of knowledge, and mold their sentiment
Editorial content: literature; children's contributions

Baby Pictorial was founded in 1981 by the editorial department of *Little Friends*. In 1989, an independent editorial department was formed for *Baby Pictorial*.

Little Friends

Publisher: Juvenile and Children's Publishing House
P.O. Box 2820 (Book Code No. M114)
Beijing
People's Republic of China

For ages 3 to 8
12 issues per year
300,000 to 1,000,000 copies sold per issue
Format: 20 pages; full color; 18.4 x 20.8 cm; stapled
Editor-in-Chief: Chen Bo Chui
Art Directors: Xue Rong, Wang Jie
Editorial mission: to help children widen their field of vision,
inspire wisdom, and broaden their scope of knowledge
Editorial content: literature; children's contributions and letters

Little Friends was initiated in 1922 as a weekly periodical by Li Jin
Hui of the Shanghai Zhong Hua Publishing House. Today, the
magazine is published by the Juvenile and Children Publishing
House and serves preschoolers and primary school children.

Science Magazine for Juveniles

Publisher: Juvenile and Children's Publishing House
1538 Yan An Xi Road
Shanghai
People's Republic of China

For ages 10 to 15
100,000 copies sold per issue
Format: 96 pages; black and white; 13 x 18.25 cm; perfect-bound
Editor-in-Chief: Zhou Shenpei
Editorial mission: to introduce the latest science news and achieve-
ments to children
Editorial content: science, nature, education, sports, crafts, comics,
science fiction, and puzzles; children's contributions and letters

Wang Tingyun founded *Science Magazine for Juveniles* in
1976.

Baby's Pictorial

Publisher: China Children's Publishing House
No.21, Lane 12, Dongsi
Beijing
People's Republic of China

For ages 1 to 3
200,000 copies sold per issue
Format: 20 pages; full color; 18.5 x 20.4 cm; stapled
Editor-in-Chief: Wu Jianzhong
Editorial content: education, art, cartoons

Baby's Pictorial started publication in 1985 and is a government-owned publication.

Preschool Pictorial

Publisher: China Children's Publishing House
No. 21, Lane 12, Dongsi
Beijing
People's Republic of China

For ages 4 to 6
12 issues per year
400,000 copies sold per issue
Format: 16 pages; full color; 18.5 x 23.8 cm; stapled
Editor-in-Chief: Wu Jianzhong
Editorial mission: to help parents provide their children with a better education
Editorial content: literature, fantasy, nature, education, crafts, cartoons, games; children's art

Preschool Pictorial is a government-owned publication which was founded in 1982.

Children's Literature

Publisher: China Children's Publishing House
No. 21, Lane 12, Dongsi
Beijing
People's Republic of China

For ages 10 to 16
12 issues per year
100,000 copies sold per issue
Format: 144 pages; black and white; 13 x 18.3 cm; perfect-bound
Editor-in-Chief: Wang Yidi
Editorial mission: to cultivate children's literary and aesthetic appreciation and to acquaint them with all kinds of literary genres
Editorial content: literature, art; children's contributions and letters

Children's Literature is a government-owned publication which was founded in 1963. It is the nation's most influential and authoritative literary magazine for children.

Chinese Children

Publisher: China Children's Publishing House
No. 21, Lane 12, Dongsi
Beijing
People's Republic of China

For ages 6 to 9
12 issues per year
150,000 copies sold per issue
Format: 16 pages; 18.5 x 25.5 cm; full color; stapled
Editor-in-Chief: Yan Zhenguo
Editorial content: literature, nature, history, science fiction, education, art, sports, comics, puzzles; children's contributions and letters

Chinese Children was founded in 1972 and is a government-owned publication.

Middle School Students

Publisher: China Children's Publishing House
No. 21, Lane 12, Dongsi
Beijing 100708
People's Republic of China

For ages 12 to 16
12 issues per year
350,000 copies sold per issue
Format: 64 pages; black and white; 13 x 18.3 cm; stapled
Editor-in-Chief: Liu Xiliang
Editorial content: literature, nature, science, history, education,
social science, sports, crossword puzzles; children's contributions
and letters

Middle School Students is a government-owned publication which
was founded in 1930.

We Love Science

Publisher: China Children's Publishing House
No. 21, Lane 12, Dongsi
Beijing 100708
People's Republic of China

For ages 10 to 15
12 issues per year
80,000 copies sold per issue
Format: 32 pages; black and white; 18.5 x 25.5 cm; stapled
Editor-in-Chief: Yu Jun-xiong
Editorial mission: to provide a publication for children who like
natural science
Editorial content: fantasy, nature, science, science fiction, education, anthropology, cartoons; children's contributions and letters

We Love Science is a government-owned publication which was
founded in 1960.

Children's Scientific Pictorial

Publisher: Jiangsu Juveniles' and Children's
Publishing House
56 Gaoyunling
Nanjing
People's Republic of China

For ages 7 to 11
6 issues per year
80,000 copies sold per issue
Format: 24 pages; full color; 19 x 17 cm; stapled
Editor-in-Chief: Xu Jingdong
Art Directors: Wang Lie, Wang Zumin
Editorial mission: to spread scientific knowledge
among children and to develop their intelligence
Editorial content: science; children's art and letters

Founded in 1980 by Xue Xue under the name *Golden
Key,* the government-owned magazine was renamed
Children's Scientific Pictorial in 1986. Its mascot is a
boy named Keke.

Weilai

Publisher: Jiangsu Juveniles' and Children's
Publishing House
56 Gaoyunling
Nanjing
People's Republic of China

Format: 192 pages; black and white;
18.5 x 26 cm; perfect-bound

For the Children

Publisher: Modern Family for Children's Magazines
No. 7, Lane 101, Song Shan Road
Shanghai
People's Republic of China

For ages 0 to 14
12 issues per year
200,000 copies sold per issue
Format: 32 pages; black and white; 18.5 x 26 cm; stapled
Editors: Ye Guoqiang, Sun Xiaoqi
Editorial mission: to emphasize home education and coordinate
the relation between home, school, and society
Editorial content: education; children's letters

For the Children started publication in 1982 and was nominated one
of the ten best magazines of Shanghai in 1988.

Good Child

Publisher: Juvenile Press Agency
500 Shan Xi Road (N.)
Shanghai 200041
People's Republic of China

For ages 4 to 16
12 issues per year
180,500 copies sold per issue
Format: 14 pages; full color; 19 x 25.8 cm; stapled
Editor-in-Chief: Li Ren Xiao
Art Director: Mao Yong Kun
Editorial Content: literature; children's contributions

Good Child, a government-owned publication, was founded by Li
Ren Xiao in 1969.

Orient Juvenile

Publisher: The Magazine Orient Juvenile
No. 7 West Chank An Street
Beijing
People's Republic of China

For ages 10 to 15
12 issues per year
100,000 copies sold per issue
Format: 48 pages; black and white; 18.5 x 26 cm; stapled
Editors: Hao Yan, Zhao Jin-ju, Gao Yu-kun
Art Director: Liang Yi-fan
Editorial mission: to heighten children's knowledge of languages
and literature and to develop their writing technique
Editorial content: literature; children's contributions and letters

Orient Juvenile was founded in 1982 by the Beijing Federation of
Literary and Arts Circle.

Story Pictorial

Publisher: People's Fine Arts Publishing House
Bei Zong Bu 32
Beijing
People's Republic of China

For ages 6 and up
12 issues per year
260,000 copies sold per issue
Format: 56 pages; black and white; 18.5 x 26 cm; stapled
Editor-in-Chief: Meng Qing Tiang
Art Director: Zhang Qing
Editorial mission: to broaden children's knowledge by providing
them with reading material and entertainment
Editorial content: art, stories; children's art and letters

Founded in 1951 by Zou Ya, *Story Pictorial,* a government-owned
publication, was the first fine arts magazine published after the
founding of the People's Republic of China. It reflects both the
nation's history and current life.

Storyteller

Publisher: Shanghai Literary and Art Publishing House
Shao-xin Road 74
Shanghai
People's Republic of China

For ages 8 to 25
12 issues per year
Format: 64 pages; black and white; 13 x 18.5 cm; stapled
Editor-in-Chief: He Cheng-wei
Art Director: Li Bao-qiang
Editorial content: literature; children's stories and letters

Storyteller was founded in 1963 by Li Zhong-fa, Qian Xun-juan, and the Shanghai Literary and Art Publishing House.

The Teenagers

Publisher: The Writers' Association of Guangdong
75 Wende Lu
Guangzhou
People's Republic of China

For ages 13 to 18
6 issues per year
320,000 copies sold per issue
Format: 48 pages; black and white; 18.5 x 25.75 cm; stapled
Editor-in-Chief: Huang Qingyun
Art Director: Huang Jia Wen
Editorial mission: to be an intimate friend to youngsters
Editorial content: general interest; children's contributions and
letters

Founded in 1987 by Huang Qingyun, *The Teenagers* is a nonprofit
publication owned by The Writers' Association of Guangdong.

Teenagers in China and Abroad

Publisher: Guangxi People's Publishing Collective
Nanning
Guangxi Province
People's Republic of China

For ages 12 to 17
Format: 48 pages; black and white; 18.5 x 26 cm; stapled
Editor-in-Chief: Li Yun Kwan
Art Director: Kuo Liang

Teenagers in China and Abroad was first published in 1983.

Young Pioneers

Publisher: Young Pioneers Magazine
1, Sibeitongjin, Dongshan
Guangzhou
People's Republic of China

For ages 9 to 13
12 issues per year
700,000 copies sold per issue
Format: 32 pages; black and white; 13 x 18.51 cm; stapled
Editors: Jiang Guo-feng, Li Yan-hui
Art Director: He Ting-jin
Editorial content: general interest; children's contributions and
letters

Young Pioneers, a school publication, was founded in 1956 by
Huang Qing-yun.

FAR EAST
ASIA

HONG
KONG

Little Red Apple

Publisher: Le Grain De Seneve Publishing Co. Ltd.
1802 Hopewell Centre, 183 Queens Road East
Hong Kong

For ages 3 to 6
12 issues per year
Format: 24 pages; full color; 20.75 x 23.5 cm; stapled
Editor-in-Chief: H.Y. Leung
Art Director: T.N. Lam
Editorial mission: to stimulate learning, understanding, and play
Editorial content: general interest, parents' section

Little Red Apple was founded in 1977 by Fr. B. Petit.

Red Apple

Publisher: Le Grain De Seneve Publishing Co. Ltd.
1802 Hopewell Centre, 183 Queens Road East
Hong Kong

For ages 6 to 8
12 issues per year
Format: 28 pages; full color; 20.75 x 23.5 cm; stapled
Editor-in-Chief: H.Y. Leung
Art Director: T.N. Lam
Editorial mission: to stimulate learning, understanding, and play
Editorial content: general interest, parents' section

Red Apple was founded in 1977 by Fr. B. Petit.

White Antelope

Publisher: Le Grain De Seneve Publishing Co. Ltd.
1802 Hopewell Centre, 183 Queens Road East
Hong Kong

For ages 8 to 12
12 issues per year
Format: 24 pages; full color; 20.5 x 27.5 cm; stapled
Editor-in-Chief: H.Y. Leung
Art Director: T.N. Lam
Editorial mission: to stimulate learning, understanding, and play
Editorial content: general interest

White Antelope was founded in 1977 by Fr. B. Petit.

Champak

FAR EAST
ASIA

INDIA

Publisher: Delhi Press Ratra Prakashan Ltd.
E-3, Jhandewala Estate
New Delhi 110055
India

For ages 4 to 10
24 issues per year
1,000,000 copies sold per issue
Format: 64 pages; full color; 13.5 x 20 cm; stapled
Editor-in-Chief: Vishwa Nath
Editorial mission: to give modern, purposeful, and entertaining
reading material to young children
Editorial content: literature, comics; children's contributions and
letters

Champak was founded in 1968 by Vishwa Nath as a 32-page
monthly. As its circulation grew, color and pages were added and
the publication became a semimonthly. Cheeka, a fictional rabbit,
has a new adventure in every issue.

Children's World

Publisher: Children's Book Trust, New Delhi
Nehru House
New Delhi 110002
India

For ages 6 to 16; typical reader is 8 to 13
12 issues per year
20,000 copies sold per issue
Format: 64 pages; black and color; 18 x 24.5 cm; stapled
Editor-in-Chief: K. Ramakrishnan
Art Director: Subir Roy
Editorial mission: to stimulate the latent creative talents in
children and to encourage them to read
Editorial content: general interest; children's contributions and
letters

Children's World was founded in 1968 by K. Shankar Pillai as an
offshoot of Shankar's International Children's Competition. It is
written in English and funded by the Children's Book Trust. A
character named Perky appears regularly in the magazine.

Junior Quest

Publisher: B. Viswanatha Reddi
Dolton Agencies, Chandamama Buildings
Vadapalani
Madras - 600026
India

For ages 8 to 16
12 issues per year
5,800 copies sold per issue
Format: 56 pages; black and color/full color pages; 20.2 x 27.2 cm;
stapled
Managing Editor: B. Viswanatha Reddi
Designer: Deepa Kamath
Editorial mission: to package information as fun in order to make
it appealing to children
Editorial content: general interest, wildlife, history; children's
contributions and letters

Junior Quest was started in 1989 to provide children with English
reading material that varies from that used in school and to help
encourage children to use the magazine as a source of information as
opposed to television. Its mascot is JQ, a teenage reader cartoon
figure.

Nandan

Publisher: The Hindustan Times Ltd.
Hindustan Times House, 18-20 Kasturba Gandhi Marg
New Delhi
India

For ages 7 to 16
12 issues per year
282,000 copies sold per issue
Format: 76 pages; black and color/full color sections;
17.5 x 23 cm; stapled
Editor-in-Chief: Bharti Jai Prakash
Art Director: Prashant Sen
Editorial mission: to entertain young people and to teach them the values and ideals of humanity, brotherhood, and world peace
Editorial content: literaure; children's contributions and letters

Nandan was founded by K.K. Birla in 1964. It has won a prize for excellence in printing and production from the Indian government.

Parag

Publisher: Times of India Group
10, Daryaganj
New Delhi 110002
India

For ages 8 to 16
12 issues per year
35,000 copies sold per issue
Format: 100 pages; black and color/full color pages; 14.5 x 21 cm;
stapled
Editor-in-Chief: Harikrishna Devsare
Art Director: Raj Kamal
Editorial mission: to provide readers with knowledge of modern
life, values, and scientific developments
Editorial content: general interest; children's contributions and
letters

Founded in 1959 by S.P. Jain, the chairman of the *Times of India*,
Parag is published in Hindi. It has contributed significantly to the
development of modern children's Hindi literature and is known for
its original modern literature.

Tamasha

Publisher: Katha
CII 27 Tilak Lane
New Delhi - 110001
India

For ages 10 to 14
4 issues per year
Format: 24 pages; black and color/full color pages; 17.75 x 22.75 cm; stapled
Editor-in-Chief: Geeta Dharmarajan
Art Director: Dipak Mukherjee
Editorial mission: to expose rural children to quality writing, design, and illustrations; to help them overcome stereotypical gender- and culture-biased thinking; and to teach them about health and the environment in an entertaining manner
Editorial content: health awareness, environment, literature; children's contributions and letters

Tamasha was first published by Geeta Dharmarajan in 1989. It is supported by UNICEF and is nonprofit. To date, issues have been published in the Hindi and Kannada languages. Its mascot is Tamasha the elephant. Other characters include the girl Lakshmi and Tobakachi, a demon who spreads diseases and evil ideas.

Target

Publisher: Living Media India Ltd.
F 14/15 Connaught Place
New Delhi 110001
India

For ages 8 to 14
12 issues per year
30,000 copies sold per issue
Format: 56 pages; black and color; 20 x 26.5 cm; stapled
Editor-in-Chief: Aroon Purie
Art Director: Sujata Singh
Editorial mission: to encourage a belief in democracy and social justice, a respect for different customs and beliefs, a strong commitment to the unity of India, and a scientific temper
Editorial content: general interest, literature by Indian writers; children's contributions and letters

Target was launched in 1979 by Living Media India Pvt. Ltd. as a national magazine written in English. Readers are encouraged to participate in community activities through the Target Club. Several animal characters appear regularly in the publication.

Tinkle

Publisher: India Book House Private Limited
Partha Books Division Nav Prabhat Chambers
Dadar Bombay 400028
India

For ages 8 to 14
24 issues per year
77,000 copies sold per issue
Format: 34 pages; full color; 17.5 x 24 cm; stapled
Editor-in-Chief: Anant Pai
Editorial mission: to educate through entertainment; to make science, nature, and geography more interesting by presenting them through cartoon strips
Editorial content: fantasy, nature, science, education, astronomy, crafts, puzzles; children's contributions and letters

Tinkle started publication in 1980 as a monthly.

Takusan no Fushigi
(A World of Wonder)

Publisher: Fukuinkan Shoten
6-6-3 Honkomagome, Bunkyoku
Tokyo 113
Japan

For ages 8 to 12
12 issues per year
61,000 copies sold per issue
Format: 40 pages; full color; 19 x 25 cm; stapled
Editor-in-Chief: N. Kanou
Art Director: S. Horiuchi
Editorial mission: to encourage schoolchildren to observe the
world and its wonders
Editorial content: general interest

Takusan no Fushigi was started by A. Saito and N. Kanou in 1985.

Kagaku no Tomo (Children's Science Companion)

Publisher: Fukuinkan Shoten
6-6-3 Honkomagome, Bunkyoku
Tokyo 113
Japan

For ages 4 to 7
12 issues per year
231,000 copies sold per issue
Format: 28 pages; full color; 22.5 x 25 cm; stapled
Editor-in-Chief: H. Takeda
Editorial mission: to stimulate and cultivate children's curiosity about natural science and the world around them
Editorial content: nature, science, astronomy, social science; children's letters

Kagaku no Tomo was started by T. Mastui in 1969 to provide suitable reading material that focuses on natural science, social science, geography, history, and other "world wonders." It is enjoyed by adults as well as children.

Kodomo no Tomo (Children's Companion)

Publisher: Fukuinkan Shoten
6-6-3 Honkomagome, Bunkyoku
Tokyo 113
Japan

For ages 4 to 7
12 issues per year
20,000 copies sold per issue
Format: 32 pages; full color; 19 x 26 cm; stapled
Editor-in-Chief: Y. Kawasaki
Editorial mission: to provide quality illustrated stories which children can enjoy repeatedly
Editorial content: literature; children's letters

Kodomo no Tomo was started by T. Matsui in 1956. Its principle has not changed since the first issue. One writer and one illustrator—both national—team up to produce each issue in a highly artistic style. Each issue contains a single quality illustrated story.

Kobotachi

Publisher: The Editorial Office of Kobotachi
500 Mieji-Cho 1-27
Gifu-city
Japan

For ages 5 to 12
12 issues per year
6,000 copies sold per issue
Format: 48 pages; black and color; 18 x 28.7 cm; stapled
Editor-in-Chief: Raikyo Suzuki
Art Director: Hideo Kunieda
Editorial mission: to provide environmental education and quality
reading material, to recommend good books, and to publish children's contributions
Editorial content: general interest, all original stories, illustrations,
photographs; children's contributions and letters

Kobotachi was first published in 1974 by Eizou Kunieda and the
Association of Juvenile Literature. Circulation grew to 10,000
within a few years, but has declined in recent years.

FAR EAST
ASIA

KOREA

Haksaeng Kwahak
(Students' Science)

Publisher: Chang Kang Chae
14 Chunghak-dong Chongro-ku
Seoul
Korea

For ages 10 to 15
12 issues per year
120,000 copies sold per issue
Format: 324 pages; black and color/full color sections; 18.6 x 25.75 cm; perfect-bound
Editor-in-Chief: Choi Soon Shik
Art Director: Chun Chae Won
Editorial mission: to provide science material for children
Editorial content: science, science fiction, fantasy, education, astronomy, sports, puzzles; children's letters

Haksaeng Kwahak was started by Chang Kang Chae in 1965.

Pioneriin Udirdagch
(Pioneer Leader)

Publisher: Central Committee of Mongolian Revolutionary Youth
Ulan Bator
Mongolia

For ages 9 to 12; typical reader is a member of the Mongolian
Pioneer Organization
4 issues per year
Format: 48 pages; black and white; 17 x 25.5 cm; stapled
Editor-in-Chief: D. Nyamaa
Art Director: D. Puschkin

Pioneriin Udirdagch was first published in 1980.

Pioneriin Unen
(Pioneer Truth)

Publisher: Central Committee of
Mongolian Revolutionary Youth
Ulan Bator
Mongolia

For ages 8 to 14; typical reader is a youth organization
member
6 issues per year
Format: 16 pages; black and white; 29.5 x 42 cm;
unbound

Pioneriin Unen was first published in 1943.

Zalgamzhlagch
(The New Generation)

Publisher: Central Committee of
Mongolian Revolutionary Youth
Ulan Bator
Mongolia

For ages 6 to 8; typical reader is a youth organization
member
4 issues per year
Format: 48 pages; black and white/black and color
pages; 21.5 x 26 cm; stapled
Editor-in-Chief: D. Nyamaa
Art Director: D. Puschkin

Zalgamzhlagch was founded in 1926.

Bookworm Digest

FAR EAST ASIA

SINGAPORE

Publisher: Bookworm Consultants Pte. Ltd.
257 Selegie Road, #11-275 Selegie Complex
Singapore 0718
Singapore

For ages 9 to 14
5 issues per year
33,500 copies sold per issue
Format: 36 pages; black and color; 21 x 27.6 cm; stapled
Editor-in-Chief: David Chong Tat Chong
Art Director: David Chong Tat Chong
Editorial mission: to encourage children to read and to make reading fun
Editorial content: education, jokes, general knowledge, space news; children's contributions and letters

Bookworm Digest was founded in 1985 by David Chong Tat Chong. It is written in English and its mascots are bookworm characters.

Funland

Publisher: Wixard Publishers Pte. Ltd.
625 Aljunied Road, # 05-07 Aljunied Industrial Complex
Singapore 1438
Singapore

For ages 9 to 13; typical reader is 11
16,800 copies sold per issue
Format: 32 pages; black and white; 21.5 x 29 cm; stapled
Editor-in-Chief: Bernard Lee
Art Director: C.S. Ong
Editorial mission: to entertain and educate
Editorial content: general interest; children's contributions and
letters

Funland was started by Bernard Lee when he retired from teaching
in 1985 in order to "keep his mind busy." The magazine is written
in English and has an owl as a mascot.

Singapore Scientist

Publisher: Singapore Science Centre
Science Centre Road
Singapore 2260
Singapore

For ages 10 to 25
4 issues per year
22,200 copies sold per issue
Format: 70 pages; black and color/full color section; 20.5 x 29.5 cm; stapled
Editor-in-Chief: Foo Tok Shiew
Art Directors: Clarence Sirisena, Ong Chieng Yin
Editorial mission: to educate readers in science and technology
Editorial content: science; readers' contributions and letters

Singapore Scientist is an English-language publication that was started in 1974 by the Singapore Science Centre.

Young Generation

Publisher: EPB Publishers Pte. Ltd.
Blk 162, Bukit Merah Central #04-3545
Singapore 0351
Singapore

For ages 5 to 14
12 issues per year
33,000 copies sold per issue
Format: 40 pages; black and color/full color section; 19.5 x 27 cm;
stapled
Editor-in-Chief: Clarence Lim
Editorial mission: to educate, inform, and entertain young readers
Editorial content: stories, cartoons, funny facts, contests, poems,
science, geography, history, wildlife, famous people; children's
contributions and letters

Young Generation was founded by EPB Publishers in 1980. It is the
only bilingual (English/Chinese) children's magazine in Singapore.
Its mascots are Vinny the Little Vampire, Pip the Pilot, and Con-
stable Acai.

Zoo-Ed

Publisher: Singapore Zoological Gardens
80 Mandai Lake Road
Singapore 2572
Singapore

For ages 8 to 13
4 issues per year
140,000 copies sold per issue
Format: 12 pages; black and white/full color section; 22 x 35 cm; unbound
Editor-in-Chief: Ong Swee Law
Editorial mission: to educate readers in the life sciences
Editorial content: science, endangered species, conservation; original articles, illustrations and photographs; children's contributions

Zoo-Ed was started by Ong Swee Law in 1979. It is a zoo publication written in English. Most of its subscriptions are sold through schools. O.T. the otter is its mascot.

FAR EAST ASIA

TAIWAN

Children's Magazine

Publisher: Children's Book Publishing Programme of the Taiwan Provincial Department of Education
2th F, 172 Chung-Hsiao E. Road, Section 1
Taipei
Taiwan, Republic of China

For ages 6 to 12
12 issues per year
50,000 copies sold per issue
Format: 104 pages; 19 x 26 cm; full color; perfect-bound
Editor-in-Chief: Ho Chen-Kuang
Art Director: Ho Chen-Kuang
Editorial mission: to improve children's education, to enrich their life experiences, to cultivate their imaginations, and to beautify their minds
Editorial content: general interest; children's contributions and letters

Dr. Ling Ching-Chiang, the former Director of the Taiwan Provincial Department of Education, founded *Children's Magazine* in 1986 to provide extracurricular reading material for elementary school-children.

Copel Science Magazine

Publisher: New-Schoolmate's Book Co.
6F, 501 Tun-Hwa S. Road
Taipei
Taiwan, Republic of China

For ages 9 to 15
12 issues per year
70,000 copies sold per issue
Format: 116 pages; full color; 21 x 27.5 cm; perfect-bound
Editor-in-Chief: Shu-Wei Fan
Art Director: Jy-Fan Chen
Editorial mission: to teach children new science concepts through easy reading
Editorial content: science; children's contributions and letters

President Jiung-Konq Liaw founded *Copel Science Magazine* in 1985. Caricatures of a rabbit and a mechanical dog greet readers every month.

Little Newton Magazine

Publisher: Newton Publishing Company, Ltd.
1F No. 25, Lane 107, Sec 2, Ho-Ping E Rd.
Taipei
Taiwan, Republic of China

For ages 6 to 15
12 issues per year
60,000 copies sold per issue
Format: 96 pages; full color; 21.5 x 27 cm; perfect-bound
Editor-in-Chief: Kao Yuan-Ching
Art Director: Liu Chou-Ling
Editorial mission: to approach children's graphic science publications in a new way, to cultivate the proper approach to scientific study, and to offer a wide range of source materials
Editorial content: nature, science; children's contributions and letters

Little Newton was founded in 1984 by Kao Yuan-Ching. The undisputed quality of its articles and illustrations has made the magazine a popular science publication for children in Taiwan.

Seedling

Publisher: Seedling
Fl 17. No. 522 Min Chyuan E. Road
Taipei
Taiwan, Republic of China

For ages 3 to 8
12 issues per year
Format: 48 pages; black and color/full color sections; 21 x 28 cm;
stapled
Editor-in-Chief: Ling-Huei Hsu
Art Director: Liang-Hwa Shen
Editorial mission: to help children explore the world through
literature and science and to give them activities which will help
them form concepts
Editorial content: literature, fantasy, nature, science, science
fiction, education, art, social science, sports, crafts, puzzles

Seedling was first published in 1977 as part of a newspaper. Color
was added in 1978.

Wisdom

Publisher: Taiwan Television Culture Enterprises Co.
11A Floor 2 Pa Tea Road, Section 3
Taipei
Taiwan, Republic of China

For ages 8 to 12
12 issues per year
45,000 copies sold per issue
Format: 130 pages; black and color/full color section; 18.4 x 25.9 cm; perfect-bound
Editor-in-Chief: Kuan-Yueh-Shu
Art Director: Kuan-Yueh-Shu
Editorial mission: to give children wisdom and warmth
Editorial content: general interest; children's contributions and letters

Stone K. Shik founded *Wisdom* in 1985.

Youth Juvenile Monthly

Publisher: Youth Cultural Enterprise Co., Ltd.
3rd Fl. 66-1. Sec. 1. Chung-Ching S. Rd.
Taipei
Taiwan, Republic of China

For ages 12 to 18
12 issues per year
Format: 112 pages; black and color/full color section; 19 x 26 cm;
perfect-bound
Editor-in-Chief: Hsiao-Ying Sun
Art Directors: Pei Huey Jin, Ju Suh Fang
Editorial content: general interest; children's contributions and
letters

Song Shyr Sheuan founded *Youth Juvenile Monthly* in 1976.

FAR EAST
ASIA

THAILAND

Chaiyapruk Cartoon

Publisher: Thai Watana Pamt Co., Ltd.
599 Maitrichit Road
Bangkok
Thailand

For ages 6 to 12
12 issues per year
50,000 copies sold per issue
Format: 48 pages; black and color; 21 x 29.5 cm; stapled
Editor-in-Chief: Narong Prapasanobon
Art Director: Narong Prapasanobon
Editorial mission: to provide moral education and to entertain
Editorial content: cartoons, stories; children's contributions and letters

Chaiyapruk Cartoon was begun by Narong Prapasanobon in 1977. The magazine is sold at a very low price in order to make it available to poor children in rural areas. Its mascots are Tarzan and his monkey.

AUSTRALASIA

AUSTRAL-ASIA

AUSTRALIA

Eyespy

Publisher: Ashton Scholastic Pty Ltd.
P.O. Box 597
Gosford NSW 2259
Australia

For ages 8 to 12
6 issues per year
Format: 32 pages; full color; 27.5 x 20.6 cm; stapled
Editor-in-Chief: David Harris
Art Director: Debbie Brown
Editorial mission: to present environmental and natural science to children in an interesting and informative way
Editorial content: nature; children's contributions and letters

Eyespy was founded by Ashton Scholastic in 1983. The Eyespy Gang and Chris the Frog are the magazine's mascots.

Lucky

Publisher: Ashton Scholastic Pty Ltd.
P.O. Box 579
Gosford NSW 2250
Australia

For ages 5 to 7; typical reader is 6
6 issues per year
Format: 32 pages; full color; 27.5 x 20.6 cm; stapled
Editor-in-Chief: David Harris
Art Director: Debbie Brown
Editorial mission: to reinforce skills while entertaining
Editorial content: crafts, jokes; children's contributions and letters

Lucky was founded by Ashton Scholastic in 1986. The magazine's
mascots include Lucky cat and friends.

Puffinalia

Publisher: The Australian Puffin Club
P.O. Box 257
Ringwood, VIC 3143
Australia

For ages 6 to 16
4 issues per year
10,000 copies sold per issue
Format: 32 pages; black and white; 16.2 x 23.2 cm; stapled
Editor-in-Chief: Sandra Thorogood
Editorial mission: to encourage children to read and to promote good literature
Editorial content: literature, book reviews; children's contributions and letters

The Australian Puffin Club was founded by Pam Sheldrake in 1977 based on The Puffin Club that had been started by Kaye Webb in England in the 1960s. *Puffinalia* is a nonprofit magazine. Muddlepup, a puffin, is its mascot.

Bobo

Jl. Gajah Mada 110
Jakarta
Indonesia

Format: 34 pages; full color/black and white; 21.5 x 27.5 cm;
stapled
Editorial content: stories, comics, puzzles

AUSTRAL-ASIA

NEW ZEALAND

School Journal

Publisher: Learning Media, Ministry of Education
P.O. Box 3293
Wellington
New Zealand

For ages 7 to 13
15 issues per year
Format: 32 to 64 pages per issue; full color; 14.5 x 21 cm. (Parts 1-3); 17.5 x 24 cm. (Part 4); stapled
Editor-in-Chief: Barbara Mabbett
Art Directors: Lynette Vondruska, Judy Shannahan, Nick Clarkson, Clare Bowes
Editorial mission: to provide material children will want to read for interest, pleasure and information; to help children understand themselves and the social and natural environment in which they live
Editorial content: literature; children's contributions

School Journal was founded by the New Zealand Department of Education in 1907 to provide instructional reading material for schoolchildren. It was issued free to all schools and used extensively in lessons. Today the mission has been broadened to include interest and entertainment in addition to instruction, but the magazine continues to be used in classrooms and is published at four different age levels.

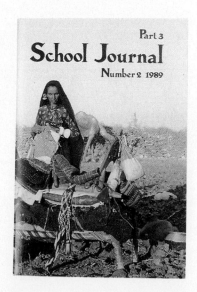

Part 3
School Journal
Number 2 1989

NORTH AMERICA

NORTH AMERICA

CANADA

Chalk Talk

Publisher: Chalk Talk Publishing
1550 Mills Road RR2
Sidney, BC V8L 3S1
Canada

For ages 5 to 14
10 issues per year
1,500 copies sold per issue
Format: 24 pages; black and white; 20.25 x 26.5 cm; glued
Editor-in-Chief: Virginia Lee
Art Director: Cynthia Barker
Editorial mission: to encourage children to read and write by giving them an opportunity to see their work in print
Editorial content: children's contributions including literature, crafts, cartoons, recipes, book reviews, and letters

Chalk Talk was founded in 1987 by Virginia Lee. It consists entirely of children's contributions and is used in classrooms across Canada. Dandy Dinosaur, the magazine's mascot, and his rabbit friends appear every month.

Chickadee

Publisher: The Young Naturalist Foundation
56 The Esplanade, Suite 306
Toronto M5E 1A6
Canada

For ages 3 to 9
10 issues per year
100,000 copies sold per issue
Format: 32 pages; full color; 21 x 27.5 cm; stapled
Editor-in-Chief: Sylvia Funston
Art Director: Tim Davin
Editorial mission: to interest children in their
environment and the world around them
Editorial content: nature, science, puzzles; children's
contributions and letters

Chickadee was founded in 1979 by The Young
Naturalist Foundation as a younger "sister" publication
to *Owl* magazine. The mascots are three little
chickadees, Dr. Zed, and Daisy Dreamer.

Owl

Publisher: The Young Naturalist Foundation
56 The Esplanade, Suite 306
Toronto M5E IA7
Canada

For ages 9 to 12
10 issues per year
100,000 copies sold per issue
Format: 32 pages; full color; 20.75 x 27.5 cm; stapled
Editor-in-Chief: Sylvia Funston
Art Director: Tim Davin
Editorial mission: to interest children in their
environment by presenting informative, stimulating, and
entertaining content
Editorial content: nature, science, puzzles, games,
contests; children's contributions and letters

Founded in 1976 by Mary Anne Brinckman and
Annabel Slaight, *Owl* is funded by The Young
Naturalist Foundation. The Hoot Club recognizes young
readers who are improving the environment. Owl, Dr.
Zed, and the Mighty Mites are the mascots.

Coulicou

Publisher: Les Editions Héritage
300 Arran
St. Lambert, QC J4R 1K5
Canada

For ages 4 to 9; typical reader is 6
10 issues per year
26,000 copies sold per issue
Format: 32 pages; full color; 21 x 27.5 cm; stapled
Editor-in-Chief: Luc Payette
Art Director: Marie-Claude Favreau
Editorial mission: to educate and entertain
Editorial content: nature, parents' corner, book reviews; children's contributions and letters

Founded in 1984 by Jacques Payette, *Coulicou* is the French version of the English Canadian magazine *Chickadee*. Its mascots are three chickadees.

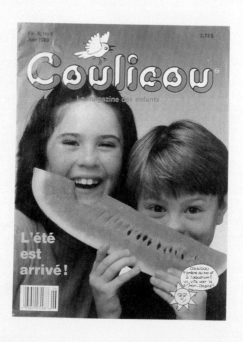

Hibou (Owl)

Publisher: Les Editions Héritage
300 Arran
St. Lambert, QC J4R 1K5
Canada

For ages 8 to 14; typical reader is 10
10 issues per year
27,000 copies sold per issue
Format: 32 pages; full color; 21 x 27.75 cm; stapled
Editor-in-Chief: Luc Payette
Art Director: Marie-Claude Favreau
Editorial mission: to educate, inform, and entertain
Editorial content: nature, science, puzzles, games; children's
contributions and letters

Hibou was started by Jacques Payette in 1980. It is the French
version of the English Canadian magazine *Owl* and is also sold in
France. Hibou-t-en-train is the magazine's mascot.

J'Aime Lire (I Love to Read)

Publisher: Les Editions Héritage
300 Arran
St. Lambert, QC J4R 1K5
Canada

For ages 7 to 12
10 issues per year
10,500 copies sold per issue
Format: 64 pages; full color; 15.5 x 19 cm; perfect-bound
Editor-in-Chief: Luc Payette
Art Director: Yves Gélinas
Editorial mission: to encourage children to love reading
Editorial content: literature, games, comics

The magazine was first started in 1978 in France. Luc Payette
founded the Canadian edition in 1987.

Je Me Petit-Débrouille

Publisher: Agence Science-Presse
4545 Avenue Pierre-de-Coubertin, C.P. 1000, Succ. M
Montréal, QC H1V 3R2
Canada

For ages 7 to 14
11 issues per year
28,000 copies sold per issue
Format: 44 pages; black and color/full color section; 21 x 27.25
cm; stapled
Editor-in-Chief: Sylviane Lanthier
Art Director: Louis Bélanger
Editorial mission: to encourage children's interest in the environment and in science methods and achievements
Editorial content: science, experiments, computers, games,
questions and answers; children's contributions and letters

Félix Maltais from Agence Science-Presse founded *Je Me Petit-
Debrouille* as a small and cheaply-typed bulletin in 1982. Its format
improved quickly and now contains many full color pages. Beppo
the frog is the magazine's popular mascot.

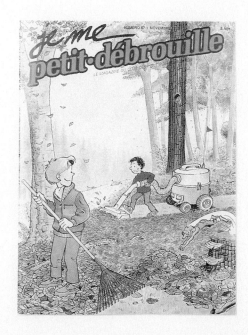

Kid Proof

Publisher: Kid Proof Publications
Box 234
Radville, SK S0C 2G0
Canada

For ages 6 to 13
2,185 copies sold per issue
Format: 12 pages; black and color; 21.5 x 27.75 cm; stapled
Editors: Lynn MacDonald, Therese Durston, Geeta McLeod,
Lynne Hall
Art Director: Claire Cilliers
Editorial mission: to encourage children to write, read, and submit
their work for publication
Editorial content: general interest, calendar of events, pets,
environment, puzzles; children's contributions and letters

Kid Proof was founded in 1987 as a whole-language publication for
elementary school children in Saskatchewan. It is used extensively
by Saskatchewan teachers and is now expanding to other parts of
Canada and the US.

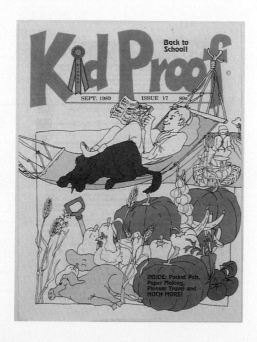

Vidéo-Presse

Publisher: Editions Paulines
3965, Boul. Henri-Bourassa Est
Montréal, QC H1H 1L1
Canada

For ages 9 to 16; typical reader is 10 to 13
10 issues per year
21,000 copies sold per issue
Format: 68 pages; full color; 21 x 27.5 cm; stapled
Editor-in-Chief: Pierre Claude
Editorial mission: to provide young people with an entertaining
and informative French Canadian magazine
Editorial content: science, wildlife, history, literature, sports,
entertainment, culture, comics; children's poems and letters

Video-Presse was founded in l971 by Pierre Guimar. At that time,
there were no French Canadian magazines for young people. Comic
characters appear every month, including Alexis le Trotteur,
Jérémie, and Robert le lézard blanc.

Boys' Life

Publisher: Boy Scouts of America
1325 Walnut Hill Lane, Box 152079
Irving, TX 75015-2079
USA

For ages 7 to 17; typical reader is an 8- to 15-year-old cub or boy
scout
12 issues per year
1,400,000 copies sold per issue
Format: 68 to 82 pages; full color; 20 x 27.5 cm; stapled
Editor-in-Chief: William B. McMorris
Art Director: Joseph P. Connolly
Editorial mission: to bring good reading to all boys and to support
the principles of scouting
Editorial content: general interest, scouting programs; children's
contributions and letters

Boys' Life was founded in 1911 by James E. West, the Chief Scout
Executive of the BSA. It is a nonprofit publication funded by the
BSA. Pedro the mailburro, a comic charater, answers readers' mail
every month.

Child Life

Publisher: Children's Better Health Institute,
div. of Benjamin Franklin Literary & Medical Society
1100 Waterway Blvd., P.O. Box 567
Indianapolis, IN 46206
USA

For ages 9 to 11
8 issues per year
Format: 48 pages; black and color/full color pages; 16.5 x 24 cm;
stapled
Editorial Director: Beth Wood Thomas
Art Director: Janet K. Moir
Editorial mission: to help children develop good health habits and
to foster in children a lifelong love of reading for pleasure
Editorial content: general interest with an emphasis on health;
children's contributions

Child Life was founded by Rose Waldo, the first editor, and the
publisher Rand McNally in 1922. It is nonprofit. The little girl
Diane and her dinosaur appear regularly in a cartoon strip.

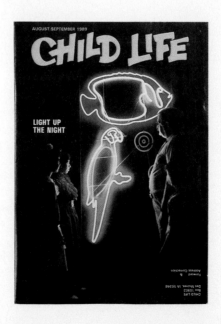

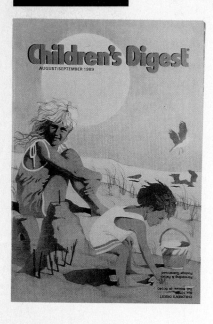

Children's Digest

Publisher: Children's Better Health Institute, div. of Benjamin Franklin Literary & Medical Society
1100 Waterway Blvd., P.O. Box 567
Indianapolis, IN 46206
USA

For preteens
8 issues per year
Format: 48 pages; black and color/full color pages; 16.4 x 23.2 cm; stapled
Editorial Director: Beth Wood Thomas
Art Director: Lisa A. Nelson
Editorial mission: to help children develop good health habits and to foster in children a lifelong love of reading for pleasure
Editorial content: general interest with an emphasis on health; children's contributions

Children's Digest was founded by George Hecht, publisher, and *Parents' Magazine* in 1950. The Mirthworms and Tim Tyme are cartoon characters that appear regularly in this nonprofit magazine.

Humpty Dumpty's Magazine

Publisher: Children's Better Health Institute, div. of Benjamin Franklin Literary & Medical Society
1100 Waterway Blvd., P.O. Box 567
Indianapolis, IN 46206
USA

For ages 4 to 6
8 issues per year
Format: 48 pages; black and color/full color pages; 16.5 x 23 cm; stapled
Editorial Director: Beth Wood Thomas
Art Director: Larry Simmons
Editorial mission: to help children develop good health habits and to foster in children a lifelong love of reading for pleasure
Editorial content: general interest with an emphasis on health; children's art

Humpty Dumpty's Magazine was begun by George Hecht, publisher, and *Parents' Magazine* in 1952. Humpty Dumpty is the mascot of this nonprofit publication.

Jack and Jill

Publisher: Children's Better Health Institute, division of Benjamin Franklin Literary & Medical Society
1100 Waterway Blvd., P.O. Box 567
Indianapolis, IN 46206
USA

For ages 6 to 12; typical reader is 8
8 issues per year
300,000 copies sold per issue
Format: 48 pages; full color/black and white section; 16.4 x 23.3 cm; stapled
Editorial Director: Beth Wood Thomas
Art Director: Ed Cortese
Editorial mission: to help children develop good health habits and to give children a lifelong love of reading
Editorial content: general interest with an emphasis on health, book reviews, jokes; children's contributions and letters

Jack and Jill was founded as a general-interest magazine in 1938 by Curtis Publishing Co. under the editorship of Ada Rose. It began evolving into a children's health publication in 1980. The Mirthworms appear regularly in a cartoon strip.

Sports Illustrated For Kids

Publisher: The Time Inc. Magazine Company
Time & Life Building, Rockefeller Center
New York, NY 10020-1393
USA

For ages 8 to 13
12 issues per year
550,000 copies sold per issue
Format: 76 pages; full color; 21.5 x 27.6 cm; stapled
Managing Editor: John Papanek
Publisher: Ann S. Moore
Art Director: Rocco Alberico
Editorial mission: to excite readers with information on professional, amateur and youth sports, using colorful photography and graphics, and to encourage participation in athletics
Editorial Content: sports, including athlete interviews, legends, fiction, sports tips, puzzles; readers' letters

Sports Illustrated For Kids was launched by The Time Inc. Magazine Company in January 1989.

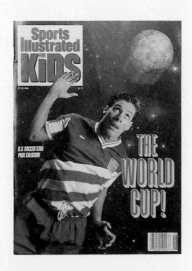

Cobblestone

Publisher: Cobblestone Publishing, Inc.
30 Grove Street
Peterborough, NH 03458
USA

For ages 8 to 14
12 issues per year
Format: 48 pages; black and white; 17.75 x 22.8 cm; stapled
Editor-in-Chief: Carolyn P. Yoder
Editorial mission: to provide children with an accurate reading
magazine that encourages further investigation on particular subjects
Editorial content: history; children's contributions and letters

Cobblestone: The History Magazine for Young People was founded
in 1980 by Frances Nankin and Hope H. Pettegrew. Ebenezer (a
man) and Colonel Cracker (a crow) appear in a cartoon strip every
month.

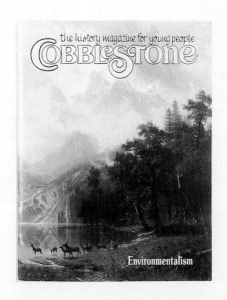

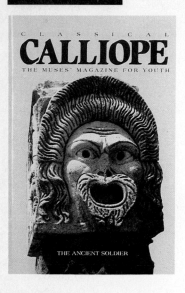

Classical Calliope

Publisher: Cobblestone Publishing, Inc.
30 Grove Street
Peterborough, NH 03458
USA

For ages 9 to 16
4 issues per year
Format: 40 pages; black and white; 15.2 x 22.8 cm;
stapled
Editor-in-Chief: Carolyn P. Yoder
Art Director: Anne Vadeboncoeur
Editorial mission: to provide children with an accurate
reading magazine that encourages further investigation
on particular subjects
Editorial content: history, classical civilization; all
original stories and articles written by the staff

Rosalie and Charles Baker founded *Classical Calliope:
The Muses' Magazine for Youth* in 1981.

Faces

Publisher: Cobblestone Publishing, Inc.
30 Grove Street
Peterborough, NH 03458
USA

For ages 8 to 14
10 issues per year
Format: 40 pages; black and white; 17.75 x 22.8 cm;
stapled
Editor-in-Chief: Carolyn P. Yoder
Art Director: Coni Porter
Editorial mission: to provide children with an accurate
reading magazine that encourages further investigation
on particular subjects
Editorial content: biography, anthropology; children's
contributions and letters

Faces: The Magazine About People was founded in
1984 by Margaret Cooper. The editorial staff works
with advisors at the American Museum of Natural
History to plan issues' contents.

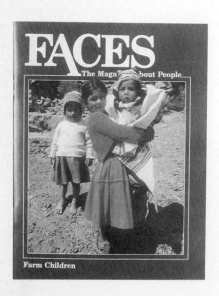

Sesame Street Magazine

Publisher: Children's Television Workshop
One Lincoln Plaza
New York, NY 10023
USA

For ages 2 to 6
10 issues per year
1,380,000 copies sold per issue
Format: 32 pages; full color; 20.5 x 27 cm; stapled
Editor-in-Chief: Marge Kennedy
Art Director: Paul Richer
Editorial mission: to educate and entertain while helping preschoolers make the transition from television to printed materials;
and to help children become aware of and sensitive to different
peoples, cultures, and careers
Editorial content: general interest; children's contributions

Sesame Street was begun by Children's Television Workshop in
1971. It comes with a separately bound, 32- to 64-page Parents'
Guide and is nonprofit. The "Sesame Street" television show
characters appear regularly in the magazine.

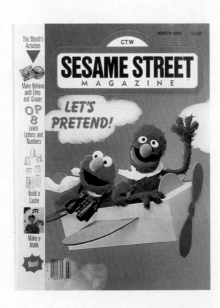

Kid City

Publisher: Children's Television Workshop
One Lincoln Plaza
New York, NY 10023
USA

For ages 6 to 10; typical reader is 7 or 8
10 issues per year
275,000 copies sold per issue
Format: 32 pages; full color; 20.5 x 27.9 cm; stapled
Editor-in-Chief: Maureen Hunter-Bone
Art Director: Michele Weisman
Editorial mission: to promote the enjoyment of reading and writing and to explore the world of children
Editorial content: general interest; children's contributions and letters

Roberta D. Miller founded *The Electric Company Magazine* in 1973 to complement "The Electric Company" TV show. The show no longer exists and the nonprofit magazine changed its name to *Kid City* to reflect its wider range of interest.

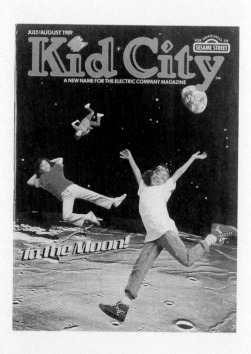

3.2.1 Contact

Publisher: Children's Television Workshop
One Lincoln Plaza
New York, NY 10023
USA

For ages 8 to 14
10 issues per year
430,000 copies sold per issue
Format: 44 pages; full color; 21.5 x 27 cm; stapled
Editor-in-Chief: Jonathan Rosenbloom
Art Director: Al Nagy
Editorial mission: to show readers that science is accessible to all, is in everything we do, and is fun
Editorial content: science, including the environment, health, medicine, math, computers, psychology, and sociology; children's letters

3.2.1 Contact was started in 1979 by Children's Television Workshop, as a companion to the television show of the same name. It is a nonprofit publication. Slipped Disk, a disk jockey who answers computer questions, is its mascot.

Cricket

Publisher: Carus Publishing Company
P.O. Box 300
Peru, IL 61354
USA

For ages 6 to 14; typical reader is 8 to 10
12 issues per year
131,400 copies sold per issue
Format: 80 pages; black and color; 17.75 x 22.8 cm; stapled
Editor-in-Chief: Marianne Carus
Art Director: Ron McCutchan
Editorial mission: to create in children a love of reading and an appreciation for good writing and illustration; to stimulate their imaginations and introduce them to the basic values of our culture and to other countries and cultures
Editorial content: literature, fantasy, nature, science, history, science fiction, astronomy, art, music, social science, sports, crafts, cartoons, puzzles; children's letters

Cricket was founded by Blouke and Marianne Carus in 1973. The publication responds to children's intelligence and does not talk down to its readers. The cartoon characters Cricket, Ladybug, and others in the Everybuggy gang appear in each issue.

Ladybug

Publisher: Carus Publishing Company
P.O. Box 300
Peru, IL 61354
USA

For ages 2 to 7
12 issues per year
Format: 40 pages; full color; 20.25 x 23.5 cm; stapled
Editor-in-Chief: Marianne Carus
Art Director: Ron McCutchan
Editorial mission: to provide sound educational opportunities for
young children and create in them a love of reading, to encourage
read-aloud sessions in families, and to develop young children's
imagination and sensibilities
Editorial content: literature, education, activities, games

Ladybug was first published by Marianne and Blouke Carus in 1990.
The characters Ladybug, Molly and Emmett, Matt and Big Dog, and
Tom and Pippo appear regularly.

DynaMath

Publisher: Scholastic Inc.
730 Broadway
New York, NY 10003
USA

For ages 9 to 13
9 issues per year
356,175 copies sold per issue
Format: 16 pages; full color/black and color; 20.4 x 27.6 cm; glued
Editor-in-Chief: Jacqueline Glasthal
Art Director: Joan Michael
Editorial mission: to help students learn mathematical concepts
and to make math a more interesting and entertaining subject for
children
Editorial content: math, education; all original articles; children's
contributions and letters

Vicky Chapman of Scholastic Inc. founded *DynaMath* in 1982 to
provide a math magazine for elementary students. The Wacky
Whimdotter family appears in every issue.

Math Magazine

Publisher: Scholastic Inc.
730 Broadway
New York, NY 10003
USA

For ages 13 to 15
14 issues per year
350,545 copies sold per issue
Format: 16 pages; full color/black and color; 20.4 x 27.6; glued
Editor-in-Chief: Tracey Randinelli
Art Director: Joan Michael
Editorial mission: to help students grasp mathematical concepts
Editorial content: math, education; all original articles; children's
contributions and letters

Maurice Robinson founded *Math Magazine* in 1980. It is distributed
through schools.

Highlights for Children

Publisher: Highlights for Children, Inc.
2300 West Fifth Avenue
Columbus, OH 43272-0002
USA

For ages 2 to 12
11 issues per year
3,000,000 copies sold per issue
Format: 42 pages; full color; 21.5 x 27.5 cm; stapled
Editor-in-Chief: Kent L. Brown Jr.
Art Director: Rosanne Guarrara
Editorial mission: to help children grow in basic skills and knowledge, creativity, the ability to think and reason, sensitivity to others, and high ideals
Editorial content: general interest; all original stories and articles; children's contributions and letters

Highlights for Children was founded in 1946 by Garry Cleveland Myers, Ph.D. and Caroline Clark Myers to incorporate Dr. Myers's principles of child development and to provide stimulating, enjoyable reading material for children. Its mascots are the Timbertoes Family and Goofus and Gallant.

Hidden Pictures

Publisher: Highlights for Children, Inc.
2300 W. Fifth Avenue, P.O. Box 269
Columbus, OH 43216-0269
USA

For ages 6 to 10
6 issues per year
160,000 copies sold per issue
Format: 36 pages; black and color/full color pages; 21 x 27.5 cm;
stapled
Editor-in-Chief: Kent L. Brown, Jr.
Art Director: Charles Cary
Editorial content: activities including hidden pictures

Hidden Pictures was started by Highlights for Children, Inc. in
1989.

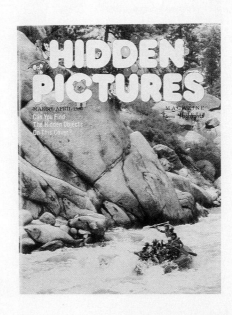

National Geographic World

Publisher: National Geographic Society
Dept. 00789, 17th and M St. N.W.
Washington, DC 20036
USA

For ages 8 to 14
12 issues per year
1,300,000 copies sold per issue
Format: 32 to 36 pages; full color; 21.75 x 27.3 cm; stapled
Editor-in-Chief: Pat Robbins
Art Director: Ursula Perrin Vosseler
Editorial mission: to diffuse geographic knowledge, to open
windows to the world for young readers, to provide them with
interesting information, and to stimulate creative thinking and
activity
Editorial content: nature, science, history, education, astronomy,
social science, sports, games, puzzles; children's contributions and
letters

World was founded in 1975 by Gilbert M. Grosvenor who hoped to
produce a magazine with a bold, fresh look designed to capture the
TV generation's attention. The text is carefully crafted to be
understandable to younger readers, but written in a no-nonsense
style that doesn't insult the intelligence of older readers.

Odyssey

Publisher: Kalmbach Publishing Co.
P.O. Box 1612
Waukesha, WI 53187
USA

For ages 8 to 14; typical reader is a 12-year-old boy
12 issues per year
101,303 copies sold per issue
Format: 40 pages; full color/black and color; 20.75 x 27.4 cm;
stapled
Editor-in-Chief: Nancy Mack
Art Director: Jane Borth-Lucius
Editorial mission: to spark young people's interest in science
Editorial content: space, astronomy; all original articles and
stories; children's contributions and letters

Odyssey was founded in 1979 by Nancy Mack and Robert Maas. A
robot named Ulysses 4-11 is the magazine's mascot.

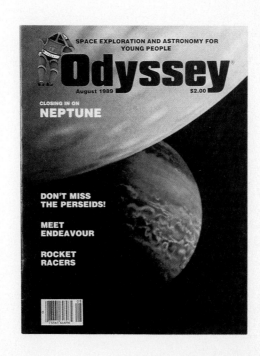

Ranger Rick

Publisher: National Wildlife Federation
8925 Leesburg Pike
Vienna, VA 22184
USA

For ages 6 to 12
12 issues per year
890,000 copies sold per issue
Format: 48 pages; full color; 20.5 x 25.5 cm; stapled
Editor-in-Chief: Gerald Bishop
Art Director: Donna Miller
Editorial mission: to inspire a greater understanding and apprecia-
tion of the natural world in a creative and entertaining way
Editorial content: nature, science, astronomy; children's letters

Ranger Rick was founded in 1967 by Trudy Farrand. It began with a
strict focus on natural history subjects and environmental problems;
its scope is broader today. Ranger Rick, Scarlett Fox, and Wise Old
Owl appear regularly in this nonprofit magazine.

Your Big Backyard

Publisher: National Wildlife Foundation
8925 Leesburg Pike
Vienna, VA 22184
USA

For ages 3 to 5
12 issues per year
Format: 19 pages; full color; 20.5 x 25.5 cm; stapled
Editor-in-Chief: Gerald Bishop
Designers: Kimberly Kerin, Mary Ann Smith
Editorial mission: to inspire a greater understanding and apprecia-
tion of the natural world in a creative and entertaining way
Editorial content: nature, science, stories, astronomy

Penny Power/Zillions

Publisher: Consumers Union
256 Washington Street
Mount Vernon, NY 10553
USA

For readers 8 to 14
6 issues per year
150,000 copies sold per issue
Format: 32 pages; full color/black and color pages; 21 x 27.5 cm;
stapled
Editor-in-Chief: Charlotte Baecher
Art Director: Rob Jenter
Editorial mission: to provide children with unbiased consumer
information, with an emphasis on decision-making skills
Editorial content: consumer skills; children's letters

Penny Power was begun by Consumers Union in 1980 as a nonprofit consumer education magazine for children. Its mascot is
Inspector Holmes. With the August/September 1990 issue, it was
renamed *Zillions,* with more pages, full color, and a new format.

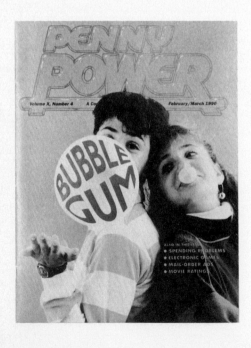

Seedling Series: Short Story International

Publisher: International Cultural Exchange
P.O. Box 405
Great Neck, NY 11022
USA

For ages 9 to 12
4 issues per year
Format: 64 pages; black and white; 13.4 x 21.5 cm; perfect-bound
Editor-in-Chief: Sylvia Tankel
Art Director: Charles Walker
Editorial mission: to promote and strengthen children's reading habits while improving international/multi-cultural understanding
Editorial content: stories portraying every aspect of the human condition in all lands and cultures

Seedling Series: Short Story International was founded by the International Cultural Exchange in 1981.

Student Series:
Short Story International

Publisher: International Cultural Exchange
P.O. Box 405
Great Neck, NY 11022
USA

For ages 14 to 17
4 issues per year
Format: 96 pages; black and white; 13.4 x 21.5 cm; perfect-bound
Editor-in-Chief: Sylvia Tankel
Art Director: Charles Walker
Editorial mission: to promote and strengthen reading habits while improving international/multi-cultural understanding
Editorial content: stories portraying every aspect of the human condition in all lands and cultures

Student Series: Short Story International was founded by the International Cultural Exchange in 1981. It publishes unabridged short stories written by living authors from all around the world.

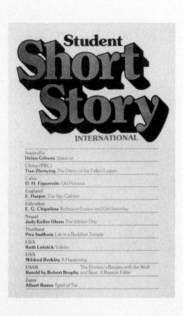

Stone Soup

Publisher: Children's Art Foundation
P.O. Box 83
Santa Cruz, CA 95063
USA

For children 14 and under
5 issues per year
11,000 copies sold per issue
Format: 48 pages; black and white/full color section; 15.25 x 22.25 cm; stapled
Editor-in-Chief: Gerry Mandel
Art Director: Gerry Mandel
Editorial mission: to encourage children to think about their lives, to observe closely the world in which they live, and to express themselves through writing and art
Editorial content: literature and art created by children, book reviews

Stone Soup, a nonprofit publication, was founded by Gerry Mandel and William Rubel in 1973. An activity guide is bound into the center of each issue.

U*S*Kids

Publisher: Field Publications
245 Long Hill Road
Middletown, CT 06457
USA

For ages 5 to 10; typical reader is 6 to 9
11 issues per year
200,000 copies sold per issue
Format: 40 pages; full color; 20.3 x 27.3 cm; stapled
Editor-in-Chief: Terry Borton
Art Director: Nancy Fisher
Editorial mission: to increase children's interest in learning and to connect them to the real world
Editorial content: general interest

*U*S*Kids* was first published in 1987. The Puzzle Squad, three girls and two boys, have adventures in every issue.

CENTRAL & SOUTH AMERICA

CENTRAL & SOUTH AMERICA

BOLIVIA

Chaski

Publisher: Luciérnaga
Casilla 3294
Cochabamba
Bolivia

For ages 6 to 14
10 issues per year
10,000 copies sold per issue
Format: 24 pages; black and color; 19 x 27 cm; stapled
Editor-in-Chief: Elisabeth Hüttermann
Art Director: Elisabeth Hüttermann
Editorial mission: to provide Bolivian children with a publication in which they can voice their opinions and express their creativity
Editorial content: literature, fantasy, nature, science, history, education, astronomy, art, music, anthropology, social science, sports, crafts, comics, puzzles; children's contributions and letters

Chaski was founded in 1982 by Centros Portales, Jesus Perez, and Elisabeth Hüttermann. It is 70% financed by European organizations in order to lower its cost to Bolivian children. Chaski, a message boy, is the magazine's mascot.

Chiquirin

Publisher: Editorial Piedra Santa
11 Calle 6-50, Zona 1
Guatemala
Guatemala, Central America

Format: 34 pages; black and color; 21 x 27.4 cm; stapled
Editor-in-Chief: Irene Piedra Santa
Art Director: Sergio Anzoátegui
Editorial content: general interest

CENTRAL
& SOUTH
AMERICA

GUATE-
MALA

CENTRAL & SOUTH AMERICA

URUGUAY

El Grillo (The Cricket)

Publisher: Consejo de Enseñanza Primaria
Bartolome Mitre 1317
Montevideo
Uruguay

For ages 10 to 12
2 issues per year
Format: 38 pages; black and color/full color section; 19.5 x 27.5 cm; stapled
Editor-in-Chief: Marta Laurino de Siola
Art Director: Washington Algare
Editorial mission: to educate
Editorial content: education

El Grillo is a nonprofit school publication which was founded in 1948 by Carlos Alberto Garibaldi.

La Nave Oikos
(The Ship Oikos)

Publisher: Consejo de Enseñanza Primaria
Bartolome Mitre 1317
Montevideo
Uruguay

For ages 9 to 15
4 issues per year
Format: 8 pages; full color; 19.5 x 27.5 cm; stapled
Editor-in-Chief: Marta Laurino de Siola
Art Director: Sergio Lopez
Editorial mission: to provide educational material for
schoolchildren and teachers
Editorial content: science

Marta Laurino de Siola founded *La Nave Oikos* in 1988.
It is a nonprofit school publication.

Moñita Azul
(Little Blue Monkey)

Publisher: Manhattan Ltda.
18 de Julio 1296 of. 102
Montevideo
Uruguay

For ages 3 to 12
22 issues per year
15,000 copies sold per issue
Format: 52 pages; full color/black and white; 19.5 x 28
cm; stapled
Editor-in-Chief: Jorge Martinez Rivas
Art Director: Pedro Cano
Editorial mission: to educate
Editorial content: general interest; children's
contributions and letters

Jorge Martinez Rivas and Raul Martinez founded
Moñita Azul in 1984.

CENTRAL & SOUTH AMERICA

VENEZUELA

Arco Iris (Rainbow)

Publisher: Neumann Foundation
Apartado Postal 3654
Caracas
Venezuela

For ages 8 to 12
10 issues per year
60,000 copies sold per issue
Format: 20 pages; full color/black and color; 20 x 29.5 cm; stapled
Editor-in-Chief: Rosa Elena Vazquez
Art Director: Mary Carmen Perez
Editorial Mission: to inform and entertain
Editorial Content: general interest, teachers' section, cooking; children's letters

Arco Iris was founded by the Neumann Foundation in 1986. It is a nonprofit publication.

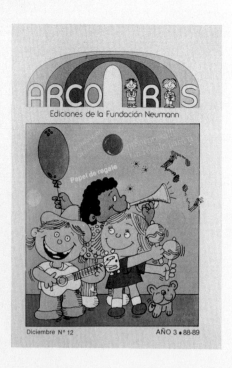

Name of Magazine

ABC, 68
ABC
   Mladych Techniku Príodovëdcu, 17
Abricot, 43
Aerostato, 61
Æskan, 69
Amico dei Fanciulli, 70
Arco Iris, 252
Asha, 133
Astrapi, 44
Ayesh, 142
Az En Ujságom, 63
Baby Pictorial, 162
Baby's Pictorial, 164
Bando, 157
Barvinok, 112
Benni, 26
Bimbo, 27
Bobo, 211
Bookworm Digest, 195
Boys' Life, 222
Camacuc, 91
Caracola, 92
Cavall Fort, 93
Chaiyapruk Cartoon, 206
Chalk Talk, 214
Champak, 181
Chaski, 248
Chickadee, 215
Child, The, 131
Child Life, 223
Children's Digest, 224
Children's Literature, 165
Children's Magazine, 200
Children's Scientific Pictorial, 169
Children's World, 182
Chinese Children, 166
Chiquirin, 249
Ciciban, 106
Classical Calliope, 228
Cobblestone, 227
Copel Science Magazine, 201
Coulicou, 216
Cricket, 232
Der Bunte Hund, 29
Diabolo, 49
Dogan Kardes, 158
Doremi, 83
Druzhba, 113
DynaMath, 234
El Grillo, 250
Eos, 37
European Language Institute, 71
Eyespy, 208
Faces, 228
Fatosi, 12
Floh, 30
Flohkiste (Grade 1), 31
Flohkiste (Grades 2 and 3), 31
Fonoun, 145
For the Children, 170
Frösi, 25
Fryske Bernekrante, 84
Funland, 196
G-Geschichte mit Pfiff, 32
Giovani Amici, 72
Good Child, 171
Gullivore, 52

INDEX

Haksaeng Kwahak, 192
Hellenic Youth Red Cross, 62
Hibou, 217
Hidden Pictures, 237
Highlights for Children, 236
Hoj, 84
Hoppla, 33
Humpty Dumpty's Magazine, 224
I.M. Italia Missionaria, 75
Il Giornale dei Bambini, 73
Il Giornalino, 74
Images Doc, 44
Ipurbeltz, 94
JP, 38
J'Aime Lire (Canada), 218
J'Aime Lire (France), 46
Jack and Jill, 225
Je Bouquine, 45
Je Lis Déjà, 53
Je Me Petit-Débrouille, 219
Jeunes Années, 52
Jumi, 99
Jump!, 56
Junge Zeit, 34
Junior Bob Magazine, 135
Junior Group Magazine, The, 134
Junior Quest, 183
Kagaku no Tomo, 190
Kamarát, 21
Kamratposten, 96
Kartinna Galerija, 15
Kavosh, 143
Keyhan Bacheha, 146
Keyhan Elmi Baraye Nowjavanan, 147

Kid City, 230
Kid Proof, 220
Kidou, 100
Kincskeresö, 64
Kipina, 114
Kirmizifare, 159
Kisdobos, 65
Klex, 13
Kobotachi, 191
Kodi, 100
Kodomo no Tomo, 190
Kolobok, 115
Kölyök, 66
Komsomolskaya Zhizn, 116
Kostyor, 117
Koululainen, 39
Krible Krable, 24
Kulanu, 153
Kulanu Alef Bet, 154
Kurircek, 107
Kushesh, 144
La Giostra, 76
La Hulotte, 54
La Nave Oikos, 251
La Rana, 77
Ladybug, 233
L'Aviöl, 101
Le Petit Ami des Animaux, 102
Leo-Leo, 92
Leppis, 40
Les Belles Histoires, 46
Little Friends, 163
Little Newton Magazine, 202
Little Red Apple, 178

Lucky, 209
Lyckoslanten, 97
Majalati, 152
Majed, 160
Malihai, 139
Materidouska, 18
Math Magazine, 235
Messaggero dei Ragazzi, 78
Middle School Students, 167
Mikado, 51
Min Häst, 98
Mis, 89
Moñita Azul, 251
Mücke, 35
Mücki, 35
Murzilka, 118
Nandan, 184
National Geographic World, 238
Ndotsi, 140
Ngouvou, 128
Noorus, 119
Norsk Barneblad, 88
Nuorten Sarka, 41
Odyssey, 239
Ohnícek, 18
Ohník, 21
Okapi, 45
Okki, 85
Orient Juvenile, 172
Ousama, 156
Owl (Great Britain), 57
Owl (Canada), 215
Panda, 79
Parag, 185

Penny Power, 242
Perlin, 53
Petit Géant, 55
PIL - Pionirski List, 109
Pilon, 155
Pimpa, 95
Pioneer (USSR), 120
Pioner (USSR), 121
Pioneriin Udirdagch, 193
Pioneriin Unen, 194
Pionieri (Yugoslavia), 108
Pionir (Yugoslavia), 109
Pionyr (Czechoslovakia), 19
Play and Learn, 58
Playpen, 130
Pomme D'Api, 47
Popi, 47
Preschool Pictorial, 164
Primavera Mondo Giovane, 80
Puffin Flight, 59
Puffin Post, 59
Puffinalia, 210
Rainbow, 132
Ranger Rick, 240
Red Apple, 179
Roshd Danesh Amouz, 149
Roshd Now Amouz, 148
Roshd Nowjavan, 150
Sadouk El Donia, 129
Sbondonics, 60
School Journal, 212
Science Magazine for Juveniles, 163
Seedling, 203
Seedling Series:
    Short Story International, 243

Sesame Street Magazine, 229
Singapore Scientist, 197
Skipper, 136
Slaveiche, 16
Slniecko, 23
Slunicko, 20
Soroush Nowjavan, 151
Spick, 103
Sports Illustrated for Kids, 226
Stafette, 27
Stezka, 20
Stip, 87
Stone Soup, 245
Story Pictorial, 173
Storyteller, 174
Student Series:
   Short Story International, 244
Süni, 67
Swiat Mlodych, 90
Syppi, 42
T-Magazine, 136
Taghna T-tfal, 81
Täheka, 124
Takusan no Fushigi, 189
Tamasha, 186
Taptoe, 85
Target, 187
Teddy, 36
Teenagers in China and Abroad, 176
Teenagers, The, 175
3.2.1 Contact, 231
Tierfreund, 28
Tina, 86
Tinkle, 188
Titov Pionir, 110

Toboggan, 49
Toktokkie, 137
Topic, 14
Toupie, 50
Trukitahed, 125
Tut, 104
U*S*Kids, 246
Vcielka, 22
Vesyoliye Kartinki, 121
Vidéo-Presse, 221
Vokrug Sveta, 123
Vyasyolka, 126
Wapiti, 50
We Love Science, 168
Weilai, 169
Weite Welt, 14
White Antelope, 180
Wisdom, 204
Yakari, 105
Young Falcon, 82
Young Generation, 198
Young Pioneers, 177
Youngtime, 138
Youpi, 48
Your Big Backyard, 241
Youth Juvenile Monthly, 205
Youth's Roshd, 151
Yuni Khudozhnik, 122
Yuni Naturalist, 122
Yuni Tekhnik, 123
Zalgamzhlagch, 194
Zillions, 242
Zoo, 98
Zoo-Ed, 199
Zornicka, 22